Tortoise

James Lewelling

ISBN 13: 978-0-9798080-2-9
ISBN 10: 0-9798080-2-2

Cover by Ellen Harvey.

Published by Calamari Press
New York, NY
www.calamaripress.com

One evening as the sun went down
And the jungle fire was burning,
Down the track came a hobo hiking
And he said, Boys I'm not turning.

—The Big Rock Candy Mountain

Ray was a patient man. He kept the most important business to himself until he was very close to the end. When he called me up, I decided to leave right away because I didn't think he had much longer. It was a long trip back and not without anxiety. I worried that maybe he had waited too long. I didn't want to get there and find him gone. I knew he wouldn't have written anything down. Or if he had, he would have compulsively edited it into a cryptic fragment that would be worse than nothing.

The drive to the airport was a straight shot. I kissed Nancy and the girls goodbye and took the elevator down to the street where a cab was waiting. There was no traffic at all, hardly unusual for that time of night. I sat beside the driver, gazing out the window at the dark blankness on my side of the road. *He wants to tell me something*, I kept thinking but couldn't get beyond that. Before I knew it, I'd pulled my suitcase from the trunk, checked myself in and was headed to the gate.

The flight was packed. It looked like every last ticket had been sold. I had to squeeze around this big beefy guy to get to my place. We were on the ground for at least a half an hour, but he didn't move a muscle. He must've been exhausted, or drunk. The stewardess had to belt him in for take off. As for me, I couldn't sleep on a plane to save my life. I held the armrests until we stopped going up. Some time after we breached the clouds, I started to relax. The beefy guy was still sleeping like a baby. I turned to the window. Below me, the world looked like surf.

Looking down on the clouds, I tried to recall what I had already heard from Ray. For a long time, the only thing I could think of was the rabbit hunt. It was a kind of festival that involved all the neighbors. They encircled a field and flushed the rabbits to the center where they clubbed them to death. Ray hadn't wanted to tell me about killing rabbits, I thought, but that was what he had. He had the death of his father too—it goes without saying. A combine killed his father. With half his body crushed under the machine, Ray's father bled to death telling other people what to do about it. He was very cool-headed, Ray said. There was also the thing about his mother, I recalled. Ray hadn't told me about it himself. Lillian told me for him. In any case, according to Lillian, Ray's mother went a bit insane shortly after Ray's birth. It had been a prolonged and agonizing delivery, and the poor woman blanked the whole thing from her mind, including Ray. When Ray was a baby—and indeed throughout his whole life— his mother never really believed that he was hers. The doctors thought a second child would bring her back to her senses. The treatment was a success in that she acknowledged the second child—a boy—all right, but she never remembered Ray. Later a soldier killed the second child—Ray's younger brother. I would say that he was killed in a war, Lillian said, but as it happened a sniper got him when he put his head up, just moments after an armistice had been declared. I don't think Ray has ever gotten over that, Lillian said.

I'm not so sure, I thought, looking down on the clouds. In fact, I couldn't think of anything that Ray hadn't gotten over, but maybe that was just because he hadn't gotten over it yet. Ray wasn't the type to talk about a problem until it had already been solved or very nearly solved. That is, he wasn't the type *to complain*. Ray always said, if you know you have something to get over, and you know what that thing is, getting over it should be a piece of cake. He was absolutely right, I thought. What's more, I thought, even in cases where you have something to get over but you don't know what it is, there's still no point in complaining. It's better to just *go with it*, as they say. There's no point in complaining about some vague, invisible thing, I thought, because, for all you know, all your complaints might be getting you under it or pushing you around it or bashing you right up against it, I thought, looking down on the clouds.

This matter with Ray must be extremely important, I thought, looking down on the clouds. He had waited his whole life to let me in on it. He wouldn't have called me if he had thought he could put it off any longer. The importance of what Ray had to tell me was directly proportional to his reluctance to do so, I thought. He wouldn't be telling me at all if he figured he could avoid it. Ray wouldn't have called if he thought someone else would tell me. Similarly, he wouldn't have called if he thought he could have told me himself but told me *later*. He was like that. If he had something important to say, he always waited until the last minute. He knew how to shut up—that's for sure.

In addition to the rabbit hunt and the death of his father, Ray had once tried to tell me about an affair he had had, I recalled looking down on the clouds. He had tried to tell me about the affair but he had been unsuccessful. At the time, I hadn't the faintest idea of what he was talking about. I only figured out that that was what he was trying to tell me years later after I had heard about it from a third party and even then I wasn't sure. I remembered his words exactly. He said, I had an affair. But at the time the words meant nothing to me. We were in a dark restaurant in the basement of the building where he worked. It was a Japanese steakhouse—the kind where they chop up your meal right in front of the table. He had invited me to dinner. He had invited me, I know now, with the intention of telling me about the affair. If he hadn't had the affair, he wouldn't have invited me to dinner. The woman with whom he had had the affair was also in the dark restaurant in the basement of the building. She was sitting at a table on the other side of the room. Ray even pointed to her, discretely, and indicated that that very woman was the one with whom he had had an affair. He said, there she is, the woman with whom I had an affair. It meant nothing to me.

Ray's erotic life, within or outside of the confines of his marriage, was completely beyond the bounds of my remotest concerns. In fact, since I was a small child, I have always found the ideas of sex and Ray as utterly incompatible. When it came time for him to tell me *the facts of life*, as they say, I didn't want to hear anything about it. Or rather I didn't want to hear anything about it *from him*. Lillian tried to help but not much. When I was very small, I must have asked her something. Maybe I'd found a tampon. Or maybe it came right out of the blue. In any case, I remember her words exactly: Every month men and women give different gifts to God, Lillian said. Women give blood, and men give urine. I hardly knew what to make of that. When I was bit older (and had ideas of my own), Ray sat me down in their bedroom and asked, do you have any questions? I had none.

The woman with whom Ray had an affair was completely unremarkable as far as I could discern. The information that he had had an affair with her took on the abstruse character of the most remote abstraction. We left the steak house without my having the slightest inkling of what had in fact taken place. But it must have been a comfort to Ray. It must have been a relief to him. At least, he thought, he knows. He knows I had an affair.

He would never have to worry about me finding out. For years afterwards, in fact up to and including the present moment, Ray has thought, he knows I had an affair. In fact, I knew nothing of the kind. Even when I did find out, from a third party, and recalled that evening in all its particulars, and it finally occurred to me that when Ray said he had an affair he had indeed *meant* that he had had an affair, I still wasn't sure. I thought, Oh *maybe* Ray had an affair after all. In fact to this day—to this very moment, I thought, looking down on the clouds—the entire matter has never assumed sufficient importance for me to conclude in my own mind whether Ray had had an affair or not.

The stewardess brought me some food. I left it on the tray. Then I unpeeled all the foil tops and looked at it. I was allergic to everything. I drank the water. The big guy sitting next to me woke up immediately. He ate his meal very quickly. After he was finished, he looked over at my tray. You can have it, I said. I can't eat it. The man nodded, and we exchanged trays so that his empty tray was in front of me and my full tray was in front of him. Then he ate everything on my tray. So now we both had empty trays in front of us. After a while, the stewardess came by and took them. I looked out the window.

I think it was Lillian, I thought, looking down at the clouds. I think Lillian convinced Ray to invite me out to dinner to explain about the affair. I think Lillian convinced Ray that I knew and further convinced him of the need to explain himself to me. I think she did it to punish him. She was the injured party after all. She was a small woman but she threw a lot of weight—especially as the injured party, *especially* with Ray. In fact if you were the injured party, it had been my experience, Ray was putty in your hands. You can bet Lillian knew this and took full advantage. And in this instance, she was the injured party *par excellence*. In

9

fact, in this instance, she didn't even need to convince Ray that I knew about the affair or convince him that I needed an explanation. She only had to say it. She only had to say, you have to tell him about your affair. You have to explain to him about your affair. In the face of this request, Ray, I am sure, was dumbstruck. It never occurred to him—as it has occurred to me, just now, sitting in this plane, looking down at the clouds—that she was punishing him. As far as Lillian's motives went, he was singularly obtuse. He might even have said to me, *Lillian thought* you should know I had an affair. In fact, that's exactly what he did say. We were sitting in the dark restaurant in the basement of the office building, and Ray said without any preamble, *Lillian thought* you should know I had an affair. And shortly afterward, as if the woman in question had walked in as a kind of visual aid, he said, there she is. That's the woman with whom I had an affair. And that was that.

He was not punished. As for me, I hadn't the faintest idea of what he was talking about. If Ray had any anxiety about telling me that he had an affair, surely that anxiety was instantly dissipated the very moment he did so. We finished our meal and spoke of other things. As it turned out, nothing could have been less punishing, for Ray, than telling me that he had an affair. Lillian, I am certain, was at home in their bedroom at that very moment, reveling in the hurt of her vindication. Lillian was sitting on the side of the bed in their bedroom at that very moment, thinking, now he's telling him. Now he's telling him that he had an affair. What's more, Lillian, sitting on the edge of their bed in their bedroom at that very moment, was thinking, now he's paying. He had an affair, and now he's paying for it by having to say that he had an affair. The hurt of the affair and the hurt she attributed to Ray making, what she thought would be, such a difficult admission twisted together in Lillian's guts like a knot being pulled tight, I thought, looking down on the clouds.

My knee was bleeding. I'm allergic to milk, among other things. Four days before the flight, I had eaten something with milk in it. As a result, the day before the flight, a patch of eczema had bloomed just to the left of my kneecap. In my sleep, the night before the flight, I had inadvertently scratched the patch of eczema causing it to bleed and then scab. My jeans had chaffed the scab on the flight and now it was bleeding again. It was bleeding a lot. The blood was soaking into my jeans and drying there. There was a dark stiff patch of blood soaked denim just above my knee. The more I bled the stiffer my jeans got and the more they chaffed. You can't put a bandage on that kind of sore. It just makes things worse. There was nothing to be done. I didn't think anyone else noticed. The guy sitting beside me had fallen asleep again. I looked out the window.

She'll be there too, I thought, looking down on the clouds. Lillian was still around. She would be in the house with Ray when I arrived to find out what he had to say. She would be in the house there with him, flitting around him like a bee around a boulder. At this point in his life, Ray had achieved the highest possible degree of immobility, but with Lillian it was just the opposite. Ray was near the end, and the closer he came, the more immobility he achieved. He had come quite a long way. Ray had put a lot behind him and with every passing minute, he put more behind him. At this point, there was far more behind Ray than could ever be in front of him. With Ray, you could tell just by looking at him, that just about everything was behind him and very little in front of him and that, in not too long, even that little bit would be behind him and there would be nothing in front of him. That would be the end.

But with Lillian it was just the opposite, I thought, looking down on the clouds. No one could be further from the end than Lillian. Unlike Ray, with every passing minute, Lillian had less and less behind her and more and more in front of her. At this point, it would be difficult to say she had anything behind her at all. Everything was in front of her and it stretched out for a long way. What's more the rate at which her past diminished and her future increased had accelerated virtually to the point of free fall. The way it was with Lillian, the future was always ballooning out toward limitlessness above and the past was flattening to virtually nothing below. Given these conditions, it was only natural that Lillian flitted about endlessly while Ray remained absolutely immobile. In any case, I would have to get past Lillian if I wanted to hear what Ray had to say.

She'll want to tell me herself, I thought, looking down upon the clouds. She wants Ray to tell her first, and then she wants me to hear it from her. She wants to tell me herself, whatever it is. As far as Lillian is concerned, it will make no difference whether she tells me what Ray has to say or he tells me himself. What difference does it make? Lillian is thinking. She will do everything she can to thwart me in what she considers a small matter. Lillian's efforts to thwart me have always been in inverse proportion to the importance she attaches to the matter in question. If it makes no difference, as far as she can tell, she insists. If it makes a huge difference, as far as she can tell, she defers. Habitually, she defers on questions of importance and insists on questions of minutia. She can't help it. It's in her blood. On the other hand, in the case of matters of extreme importance—such as the one Ray was sure to impart to me—in the case of matters of life and death, Lillian habitually defers to the first person who presents himself even if that person is an idiot, even if that person is a child. If Lillian understood the singular importance of what Ray had to impart to me and what's more, the importance of my hearing it from his own lips, I have no doubt she would instantly shrug off any impulse she might have had toward obstruction. Unfortunately, Lillian has no notion of the gravity of what Ray has to tell me to say nothing of the importance of him telling me himself. She has no notion of the gravity of the situation at all. How could she? There Lillian is flitting around in that house with Ray without the faintest notion of gravity at all. A woman like that empties everything she touches. If Ray told her and she told me, what she told me would be nothing but the shell of what Ray had told her. She would have emptied it. She would have received a message of great gravity and passed on a message with no gravity at all, I thought looking down at the clouds.

My knee itched like crazy. I tried not to rub it. I wish I had never gotten this allergy, I thought, looking down at the dark patch growing on my jeans just above the knee. I got it when I went abroad. Of course, no one really *gets* allergies, they're something you have all along. I had allergies before I went abroad but they got worse afterward. Allergies happen when your immune system goes out of whack. Mine went out of whack shortly before or shortly after I was born. I was born early. They kept me in a glass box. That's when it happened, I think. It wasn't bad. I'm not complaining. For things that can happen before you are born or shortly after you are born, allergies are virtually a bonus. I was born anyway. And when I was born, my brain was inside my head. I grew to my full height. The allergies were a nuisance more than anything else. At home, my nose ran and my lungs clogged up. When my nose ran, I wiped it; when my lungs clogged up, I sat on the couch. I could sit on the couch for hours waiting for my lungs to start working. Eventually, they always did. Lillian thought it was exercise but it wasn't exercise; it was hair—pretty much any kind of hair. In any case, she tried to keep me in. After a while, they took me to a doctor and found out it was just about everything. They found out I was allergic even to things I'd never come in contact with. When I went abroad, I came in contact with those things and the allergies got worse. Little scabs on the skin but you can't scratch them. Recently, the problem with milk showed up. It's no big deal but some things I miss. I can't eat donuts, for example. I feel like a jerk even mentioning it. I wouldn't except for my knee. The knee is no big deal but it's part of the trip. Chiefly, it wouldn't stop bleeding. Still I feel like a jerk mentioning it. I have two knees after all.

Back in the city where Nancy and the girls are, I saw this woman at the pool who had only one leg. The other leg was completely absent. It's the kind of thing you can't help but notice. Still I noticed her swimming before I noticed the absence of her leg but I remember her because of the leg. She swam laps. She was a good swimmer but walking was no picnic, I'll bet. Also I never saw anyone talking with her. She always came to the pool alone. People didn't talk to her because of her leg, I think. I didn't talk to her but I wouldn't have talked with her anyway. I had no reason to talk with her. In general, I don't talk with anyone unless I have a reason to talk with that person. Talking to someone for no reason has a way of putting me in a false position. Talking to someone with a reason in mind also puts me in a false position unless I get the reason out right away. In this case, the only reason for talking with the woman was the absence of her leg. That was a nonstarter. Missy talked with her. She's four. She talks with everyone. She doesn't need a reason to talk with anyone, and if she has one, it doesn't matter. She's four. She can introduce herself because she knows who she is. On that score, things are simpler when you are a kid. All a kid needs is a name, I thought, looking down on the clouds.

Getting past Lillian would be no problem, I thought, looking down at the clouds. I had been getting past Lillian all my life. For example, with the allergies, she was always trying to keep me in but I always managed to get out. Also there was deep water. Lillian hadn't spent much time in deep water and she was afraid of it. We lived next to a huge blue lake that terrified her. I wasn't afraid of deep water even a little bit. I could swim out hundreds of yards into water that was fathoms deep and got colder and colder with each fathom. I wasn't afraid of the deep water because I never swam *in* the deep water; I always swam *over* the deep water. I was a small, light child. I could crawl across the warm skin of the icy water like a spider. I could do that all day. Sinking was not in the picture. To swim I had to get past Lillian. Luckily there were more than a hundred stratagems for getting past her and each of them was perfectly effective. Lying, for example, was an entirely effective stratagem. The problem had always been *staying* past Lillian. When I was a kid, I got past Lillian on a fairly regular basis, but just as regularly Lillian would pop up in front of me again. This was extremely frustrating. It was the kind of thing that drives you nuts. In matters large and small, I accomplished my purposes without the hindrance of the least obstruction (on the part of Lillian) but in each and every instance, having accomplished my purpose, I was confronted with an obstruction (Lillian) *after the fact*. In fact, often if not in every case, these post hoc obstructions proved sufficient to nullify whatever satisfaction I had gained from my previous efforts. But in this instance, I thought, looking down at the clouds, having gotten past Lillian, I would learn a matter of such extreme importance from Ray—of importance sufficient to merit Ray's lengthy procrastination in imparting it—that any post hoc obstruction on the part of Lillian would dwindle to triviality in comparison. In fact, the matter that Ray was sure to relate to me would be of such extreme importance that once imparted any post hoc obstruction (on the part of Lillian) would be completely out of the question, I thought. I sat back in my seat, put on the sleeping mask and pulled it down over my eyes.

Back home, the girls are in school and Nancy is at work, I thought with the sleeping mask pulled over my eyes. Our apartment is empty and silent except for the tortoises scratching around in their tray. We got the tortoises for the girls. Of course they would have preferred kittens but kittens weren't in the cards, so they got tortoises. These tortoises scratch around whether anyone is home or not. The tray is not large, but it's big enough for the tortoises, I thought. Those tortoises can crawl around inside that tray all day long; and they do! I don't think the tortoises are smart enough to know which end is which. I think by the time Kayle, the bigger tortoise, gets to one end of the tray, she's forgotten the other end—the very end she came from, I thought. And it's the same with Lucy, the smaller tortoise. I think they think they are continually traveling in the same direction. And they keep running into each other! I thought. It's a long trip for those tortoises. It goes on day after day and for miles and miles, I thought with the sleeping mask pulled down over my eyes.

It's a drag not knowing who I am, I thought with the sleeping mask pulled down over my eyes. It's a drag but it's something I can live with. I'd been living with it for quite some time, I thought with the sleeping mask pulled down over my eyes. Besides it's not so unusual. A lot of people don't know who they are. I'm hardly alone in this, I thought. I can always tell when someone I meet doesn't know who he or she is. It sticks out like a sore thumb. You can't miss it, and it happens a lot. At least I know I don't know, I thought. It would be worse to not know you didn't know, I thought. If you didn't know who you were and you didn't know you didn't know, you were bound to think you were someone else. Something like that could go on for a long time—even forever. It wouldn't be that much different from being out of your mind. But you'd be bound to find out sooner or later. Either you'd figure it out for yourself or you'd run into the person you thought *you* were. In either case, there'd be trouble, I thought

Suddenly I remembered quite precisely the very first time I realized I didn't know who I was. What an odd thing to remember! I thought, with the sleeping mask pulled down over my eyes. I would have thought, I thought with the sleeping mask pulled down over my eyes, that there *wouldn't have been* any precise moment when I first realized I didn't know who I was. I would have thought that the realization of not knowing who you were would be the kind of thing that came upon one more gradually, like the knowledge of death. At some point you know, and when you know it feels like you've known all along. But at the same time, you know there must have been this other time— the time before you knew, but when exactly did you find out? Who can say? Nevertheless, there it was in my mind, clear as day, the precise moment. I shouldn't forget this, I thought with the sleeping mask pulled down over my eyes.

That happens a lot, I thought with the sleeping mask pulled down over my eyes. You remember something and because you remember it, you think you have it, but in fact you don't. You think because you remember something one moment, you'll be able to remember it again, pretty much anytime you feel like it. But you're wrong. You can't. There's a last time for everything—memories included. What makes matters worse is there is no way to tell. You can't tell when you are remembering something for the last time. You can't tell when you are remembering it that this *is* the last time, and you can't tell afterwards that that *was* the last time. The death of a memory by necessity goes unrecorded. Memories are buried all over the place, I thought with the sleeping mask pulled down over my eyes. We walk all over them all the time, but we don't have a clue because there's nothing there to mark the ground.

It was in a foreign country, I recalled with the sleeping mask pulled down over my eyes. I lived with this other guy—a skinny *moulay*—in this concrete apartment in a dusty town just off a highway in a desert. The *moulay* was my "teaching buddy." We were both teaching the peasants there English. It was part of a program. I had volunteered for the job. The moulay had had no choice. But really, neither of us had the faintest clue as to what we were doing there. It even became a joke between us. Often in the evenings after endless cups of tea, I recalled, the moulay and I, sitting on pillows with our backs against opposite walls, would look at each other across the concrete floor and say, what are we doing here? Then we'd laugh like crazy. It made no sense. To make matters worse, aside from the school, there wasn't much going on. Time was a big problem in that place, I recalled. I killed a lot of it wandering around looking at things.

That particular day, I recalled, the flies had woken me up early. Flies were also a big problem in that place. They were everywhere and they wouldn't leave you alone. In fact, the flies woke me up early pretty much every morning, buzzing around my head. Most mornings, I would just drape a handkerchief over my face, close my eyes and try to find my way back to sleep. In fact, I kept a handkerchief beside my pillow for just that purpose,

I recalled. But this one morning, when the flies woke me up, I had an idea. My idea was to walk all the way across the plain behind the town to the orange mountains on the horizon. Why not? I thought. It would be cool to see the mountains up close. I'll walk straight over to those mountains even if it takes me all day, I thought. I had all the time in the world. The plain was absolutely empty. I could walk in a straight line. There was nothing to stop me. I left the moulay in his room still asleep, wrapped in a blanket beside his books.

Outside the air was still cool and the shadows long and dark like puddles of night drying in streaks across the ground. I could see for miles right across the plain to the ridge of orange mountains on the horizon. I started walking. Though the plain looked empty from the town, as it turned out, it wasn't *completely* empty. In fact, as I walked I noticed the ground was covered with little runnels pretty much everywhere I looked. The rain had done it. It didn't rain much in that place, and it didn't rain often but the ground was so hard that whenever it did, the water ran and wherever it ran, it left a mark. Most of the runnels were no wider than a single drop. In the deeper ones, I noticed, there were wisps of grass, and where the runnels came together, stalks and bugs. Pretty soon, I had come across a bush and a single tree. I could hear birds singing and the buzz of insects. There was a humming in the air. It sounded like wind passing through vents. It was an odd noise. As I got closer to the tree, the humming grew louder. I realized it was coming from the leaves on that very tree. So this is the sound of the leaves rustling on a single tree, I thought.

The stewardess woke me up for breakfast. I had drifted off. For a long moment, I couldn't remember where I was. Then she set the tray in front of me. I looked at it for a while, stunned and

19

stupid. The plastic tray with the foil tops looked impossible. Where could such a thing have come from? I thought. Then I opened all the little foil packets. There was nothing there I could eat—everything was drowning in butter. I let the other guy have it, and he gave me his own empty tray. I looked up front.

They had put a map up on the screen. A tiny airplane marked our current position. It left a dotted line behind it to indicate where it had come from. The line shot off the screen near the upper right hand corner. The city where Nancy and the girls lived had disappeared some time ago. The city near where Ray and Lillian lived had not yet appeared. I looked out the window. The clouds were gone, or maybe we'd sunk below them. I could see the ground. The world was flat and brown and gridded with roads.

Ray told me something else about his father, I thought, looking down on the brown world gridded with roads. He told me about how after he had gone on to college, he came back to visit and was eager to tell his father about servomechanisms. These are control devices that let machines correct themselves. Like the grinders, say, that cut machine tools out of solid steel, for example. All you need to make a servomechanism is a couple of motors and some kind of instrument to measure speed or pressure or acceleration or what have you. Ray was pretty excited about these devices. He was excited because they were self-correcting. If one motor gets too much juice, the servo starts giving the juice to the other motor. If that motor gets too much, the servo switches back. You can bet those machine tool grinders push pretty hard on the metal they are grinding. The servomechanism makes sure that the metal pushes back (but not too much). If there were no servomechanisms, the piece of metal would move, and everything would get screwed up. At that time, servos could hold a piece of steel in place to the accuracy of one thousandth of an inch. God knows what they could do now. So, the story goes: Ray got home from college and followed his father out into this field on the farm. Then he launched into his explanation of servomechanisms. After the explanation had gone on for some time, Ray's father turned to him and said, do you see that tree there? I'm going to run a fence right from that tree over there to the other side of the field. Ray told me this story to illustrate the gulf that existed between him and his father. They didn't talk much, Ray said. They didn't talk much because the circles of Ray's concerns and his father's concerns did not intersect at even a single point. Ray has since explained servomechanisms to me at great length and on more than one occasion. It's the one thing he won't shut up about. Nancy finds Ray's mania for servomechanisms endearing. She doesn't have a father. Or rather, she had one, but he died. He fell off a horse. He divorced Nancy's mother when Nancy was a girl. Sometime after that, he married a stripper. Not too much later, he fell off the horse. He was drunk maybe. In any case, it was the fall that killed him. Nancy didn't go to the funeral. (She was far away at the time.) But now, she says, she wishes she had, I thought looking down at the brown world gridded with roads.

I started thinking about Nancy. Nancy is always complaining that I never hear a word she says, I thought, looking down at the brown world gridded with roads. She complains that I never hear a word she says even when I am standing right in front of her. She is absolutely right, I thought, but I wish she were here right now. I felt if she were with me at that moment, I would certainly hear every word and inflection quite clearly. It's funny, I thought. I'll be landing soon. I'll see Ray soon, and he's going to tell me what he has been waiting to tell me for such a long time. Lillian will be there too, flitting around, ready to obstruct me if she can. I should be thinking of them, I thought, but instead I find myself thinking of Nancy. In fact, the farther I get from Nancy, the more I think of her. At the same time, the closer I get to Ray and Lillian, the less I think of them. This is really odd, I thought. When I was close to Nancy (and far from Ray and Lillian), I always thought about Ray and Lillian, but now that I'm getting close to Ray and Lillian (and far from Nancy), I am thinking about Nancy. That's why I never hear a word anyone says, I thought. Nancy constantly complained that I didn't hear a word she said even when I was standing right in front of her. And she was absolutely right. I never did hear a word she said, *especially* when I was standing right in front of her. When I was standing right in front of her, I never heard a word Nancy said because my head was filled with thoughts of Ray and Lillian (who were far away). When I am standing right in front of Ray and Lillian, I'm sure, I won't be able to hear a word they say either because my head will be filled with thoughts of Nancy, I thought, looking down at the brown world gridded with roads.

Nancy hates Lillian, I thought, looking down at the brown world gridded with roads. And Lillian hates Nancy. Every time they see each other they fight. They fight about the things they say to each other and the things they don't say to each other. That's the way it is with them. I'd rather stay out of it, but that's pretty much impossible. Every time I try to stay out, but every time, I end up right in the thick of it. If it were an equal contest, I could stay out of it. I could let them settle things between themselves if it were an equal contest. But as it is, Nancy doesn't stand a chance against Lillian. Compared to Lillian, as far as fighting goes, Nancy is a rank beginner. Fighting with Nancy, for Lillian, is child's play. So, from Nancy's point of view, for me to stay out of it is the same as being in it but on the side of Lillian. At the same time, from Lillian's point of view, me being in it can only be me being in it for Nancy. If I stay out, I betray Nancy. If I get in, I betray Lillian. It would be flattering to think they were battling over my affections, but in fact, my affections don't enter into the picture at any point. Neither of them gives a flying fuck, as they say, about my affections as far as hating each other is concerned. They hate each other with an intimacy that excludes me. As it is, I have mixed feelings about both of them. For example, I would rather they didn't fight. I would rather they were both less prickly with each other and with everyone else. It's because they were poor. Both Lillian and Nancy were poor when they were children. Being poor can make you prickly. When you're poor, you have to keep an eye out for having your face pushed in it. You also have to keep an eye out for people taking advantage. When you are poor, other people—rich and poor—are constantly trying to push your face in it or take advantage. In some cases, they push your face in it *in order to* take advantage. In fact, whole industries are devoted to doing just that. Keeping an eye out all the time like that can make some poor people mighty prickly; it can drive others completely out of their minds. But *having been* poor is worse. Having been poor makes some people twice as prickly and the others twice as insane. After all, if you're poor, you can at least hope to get rich or at least to no longer be poor, but having been poor is something you are stuck with forever, I thought looking down at the brown world gridded with roads.

I met Nancy at school. We knew we would marry not long after we met. In fact, we knew we would marry the very moment we met. Marriage was in the cards for us. That was as plain as day. Her father was already dead but her mother and grandmother were still around and she had two brothers. She called to tell them we had met. It was an event. Shortly after that, she moved to my place, and her brother became very sick. One night, a relative called to give her the news. Nancy screamed and cried when she got off the phone. He had cancer in his blood. Hearing he had cancer in his blood was like hearing that he was going to die tomorrow. At that time, if you were a kid and they found cancer in your blood, you had an even chance, but if you were an adult—like Nancy's brother—it pretty much killed you every time. I borrowed some money from Ray and Lillian, and Nancy and I flew to the city where the hospital was. Her mother and her grandmother were there. I drove them around in Jack's car. We had to walk through the children's ward to get to her brother. There were bright pictures on the walls of cartoon characters and animals and the like. Her brother didn't look too good. He had started the treatment. At that time, the treatment was pretty severe. It had to be to kill the cancer. The idea was that the treatment would kill the cancer before it killed the patient. He didn't look too good. He was pretty thin, and they had put this plastic reservoir in his head. It was there to receive the treatment. He looked a bit scared but he kept his head. He complained about the inconvenience of it all. His wife and daughter were there too. I didn't know any of them but I knew Nancy and I knew him. I knew him instantly because he was going to die. When you meet someone on his deathbed, all bets are off. Everyone behaved very well. We were together on and off in that city for a couple of days. Nancy and I went back to school but then quit and moved to the city where the hospital was. I was sick of school for other reasons. As it turned out, her brother made it in as much as you can tell with something like that. The last time I saw him it was years after his illness had receded. He was pretty much OK, but still thin and he couldn't hit a barn with a baseball even from just a few yards away. The treatment did that.

It's funny the people you get to know and those you don't, I thought, looking down on the brown world gridded with roads. Some people I know the minute I see them. Others I have to hang around for a long time to know or at least until something happens. Still others I never know no matter what happens or how long I hang around them. There was this girl, for example. I knew from the first time she opened her mouth that I would never know her. Everything she said sounded like a lie. She said she had cancer in her blood when she was a child, for example. That's when I first heard that kids with cancer in their blood have an even chance—or at least some chance. She told me all about it, but everything she told me sounded like a lie. The cancer was the first in a long series of calamities. She told me about every one. Everything that had ever happened to her was a calamity of some sort and I didn't believe in a single one of them. As things happened, I hung around this girl quite a bit. We met in a far away place and there weren't too many other people around. We were *thrown together*, as they say. We even had sex and she got pregnant but no matter what happened I could never bring myself to believe a word she said. I'm sure now that every word she said was absolutely true but to me, at that time, everything she said sounded like a lie. All those calamities were true but to me they sounded like lies. I knew I'd never know this girl before she got pregnant, and I knew I'd never know her afterwards. As things turned out, I was absolutely right, I thought looking down at the brown world gridded with roads.

I looked up at the map. We'd been on the right continent for some time. The city near Ray and Lillian's place showed up in the lower left corner. It showed up as a big dot with a circle around it. The guy beside me had his headphones on. He might have been listening to music. Or maybe the news. He kept patting his thigh. He seemed completely oblivious to my

25

presence. As far as he was concerned, with the headphones on, I might not have been there at all. That was just the way I liked it. It was the next best thing to having the whole row to myself. I looked out the window.

Lillian will do most of the talking, I thought, looking down on the brown world gridded with roads. She always does most of the talking because of Ray's habit of extreme taciturnity. She'll do most of the talking but at least half (if not more) of what she says will be things Ray might have said if Lillian hadn't said them first. So it will be the same as if they were both talking. Half of Lillian's talking will be for herself and the other half will be for Ray. Ray will be absolutely silent. Standing right in front of me in the doorway there beside Lillian, Ray will not have to open his mouth. Ray doesn't make Lillian talk for him. She does it all by herself, and sooner or later she always says what he would have said *all by herself*. Ray, on the other hand, almost never talks for Lillian and he absolutely never talks for Lillian *all by himself*. If Ray ends up talking for Lillian it's only because Lillian made him talk for her. Actually even in those instances, it's much less a case of Ray talking *for* Lillian and much more a case of Lillian talking *through* Ray. And even then, it's very rare. She has to make him talk. She has to force him to do it. Lillian only talks *through* Ray in cases where either a) she is punishing him (as in the case of the affair) or b) she is unable to talk for herself. But it never works because Ray inevitably screws up. When she is punishing him, Ray is not punished because it never occurs to him that she is punishing him; when Lillian is unable to talk for herself, Ray inevitably so garbles the message that Lillian is forced, at some later time, to talk for herself anyway. Ray garbles the message because inevitably he never hears a word she says even when she is standing right in front of him. He doesn't hear a word she says because he is always thinking of something else. I don't have the foggiest idea of what he is thinking about, I thought looking down on the brown world gridded with roads.

What if he has forgotten? I thought, looking down on the brown world gridded with roads. Ray was sharp the last time I saw him, but he's getting on now. When people start getting on, they begin to forget. What's more, the importance of what they want to remember doesn't make a spit of difference. People who are getting on can forget *anything*. They can forget who has died for example. Other times, they forget who has been born. In either case, once they've forgotten, for the people who are getting on, it's like that thing never happened at all. If Ray has forgotten, he'll have forgotten completely, I thought. Not only will he not remember whatever it was he had to tell me, but he also won't remember asking me to come. I'll show up right out of the blue, a big surprise. If that happens, I can't mention it. It would cut half of him away to insist. But Lillian will remember. How could she forget? She was there when he called. I heard her in the background. It was the reverse of the usual situation. Normally it's Lillian who calls and Ray whom I can hear in the background. Lillian will remember the call because it was the call that she didn't make but in which she could be heard in the background. But she won't remember what Ray had to tell me. That part will be gone forever. She can't remember what he had to say because she didn't know what it was in the first place. Nonetheless, Lillian will insist that Ray remembered having called me. But it will have slipped away. It will be like a paper boat. The more you reach out for it, the more you make waves that push it away. It bobs right away on the little ripples you made reaching out for it. It will cut half of him away to insist like that, but Lillian won't be able to help herself. She can't really have the call unless Ray remembers it, but when Lillian is done insisting, the call will be even more absent from Ray than when she started. Instead it will fall between me and her. Ray's call, cut out completely from Ray by Lillian's insistence, will come to rest between Lillian and me. It will be ours, I thought, looking down on the brown world gridded with roads.

The *moulay* was the skinniest person I had ever met, I recalled, looking down on the brown world gridded with roads. I did get to know him but I didn't get to know him right away. His father was dead. His mother lived in the neatest home you could imagine amidst the rubble in the poor quarters of the old city far away. You can bet he never got enough to eat when he was a baby. Not in that house in the rubble—no matter how neat it was. He had a child's body but his face was all grown up. In fact, he was grown up. He was a sensible person. He kept his head down and did his homework. Being a moulay was a curse to him. In that country, it was dangerous to be a moulay no matter how much you kept your head down. Everything was dangerous in that country. People drove like maniacs, for example. And the food was often poisonous. But the most dangerous thing was to be noticed. The people who were noticed were picked out. The people who were picked out disappeared. Generally, soldiers did it, on buses mostly. Everyone tried to look alike or at least look like something. Like a student for example, or a butcher or a muezzin. For the moulay, the problem was not everyone could *be* a moulay. You had to be born that way. It was a kind of aristocracy. There were only so many of them. It was supposed to be a good thing, but it made it harder to keep your head down. The moulay had to keep his head twice as far down as other people who were not moulays. It was a curse. Still you could tell he was proud of it. I finally got to know the moulay when this soldier showed up at our door in the middle of the night. He just showed up and started banging on our door in the middle of the night. He was so big in the doorway and even

28

bigger when he came in. That soldier was huge, and he had a scar running from the corner of his eye all down the length of his cheek. His body threw crazy shadows all over our concrete box. You couldn't believe a person of his bulk could take off his boots or sit, in his socks, on a pillow on the floor. Where would his knees go? But he did. The skinny moulay produced tea and cookies out of the thin air on a silver platter I'd never seen before. I took my cue from him and smiled all over the place.

I never told Lillian about that, I recalled looking down on the brown world gridded with roads. I used to tell Lillian things but then I stopped because it became apparent to me that the gravity of whatever I had to say would vanish the very moment my words reached Lillian's ear. Also, generally, it got me into trouble but even the trouble failed to retain a particle of the gravity of whatever it was I said. I didn't tell Lillian about the noise from the windows, for example. I never told her about drifting off. It was when I had a friend. We had these floats. The water was far too cold to swim but it wasn't too cold to float. We floated in the sun with our feet in the icy water. We kicked out a ways and waited to drift in. The waves were going that way. The weather was hot and drowsy but the water was like ice. We could have drifted all day. The idea was to kick out a ways and then drift back in. We thought we were drifting in. We were in a state of perfect laziness. I could have drifted all day. When I looked up, the place we had drifted from was as far away as it could possibly be without disappearing altogether. I couldn't even pick it out on the shore. Everything looked the same. We started to paddle back but paddling was slow. There was a breeze. It was the breeze that had pushed us out there. The waves were no help whatsoever. It was impossible to tell with all that paddling whether we were still drifting out or paddling in. Air started falling along the big flat space of the lake. The breeze picked up.

The water became exceedingly blue. I jumped in. The shock of the cold water knocked the air out of me. The float just bobbed away. Something about the breeze made crawling across the water completely impossible. I thrashed on and on. I left my friend behind on his float. Once I was in the water, there wasn't much choice. After a while, a big kid showed up in a boat. That was a piece of luck, I thought, but in fact, he had been watching us.

Lillian did tell *me* something once though, I recalled, looking down at the brown world gridded with roads. She called me up. I was away at school. She called me up because she'd been rummaging around the attic and had found some pictures of herself in her school uniform. She was crying all over the phone. She wanted to know what had happened to that little girl. I guess the little girl in the picture had had a lot of plans and schemes but none of those plans or schemes had come to fruition. Instead Lillian had come to fruition. It was a real let down for her. It was like something died. Seeing that picture, for Lillian, was like gazing at her own corpse. She was very shaken up about it. She cried all over the phone. She kept saying, I don't know what happened to that girl, and asking, where is that girl? I don't remember precisely what I said but I'm pretty sure whatever it was sucked the last remaining particle of gravity right out of Lillian. In any case, the next time she called she was back to normal, and she's been normal ever since.

I should be able to see the city soon, I thought. When I see the city, it will be a surprise. Here I am looking for the city, I thought, looking down on the brown world gridded with roads, but nonetheless when I do see it, it will be a surprise. The city is like that. It always springs right up. It never appears gradually. If it appeared gradually, I might see just one bit of the city first and then another bit and then more and more until there it is, the whole city laid out beneath me. But it won't come to me like that. Instead one moment, I'll be looking down at the brown world gridded with roads just as I am now, I thought, and the next moment the whole city will spring up beneath me with its white towers and knotted freeways. One moment, nothing, I thought, and the next the whole thing—just as if it had been there all along.

Ali lived in the same town with me and the moulay, I recalled, looking down on the brown world gridded with roads. All three of us were there. Unlike the moulay, I knew Ali the moment I saw him. Not long after that, he invited me north to his village. We walked around all day, and in the evening, we lit a lantern in his grandfather's house and made tea. When it can't get any sweeter, you add more sugar, Ali said, making tea in his grandfather's house. You taste the tea and if it's too sweet, you add a bit more sugar and then it will be perfect, he said. His father was dead. His mother lived with Ali but for this trip she was staying in the house of an aunt. Ali was perfectly a young man. He had a girl somewhere and they corresponded secretly. He couldn't marry her but they corresponded secretly. There might be a lot of trouble if anyone found out. He didn't have any money. He hardly had enough to keep his mother. His mother was the softest woman I have ever seen. She was soft and frail and incredibly old. She worked like a dog. There was no one in our town for her to talk to. The people in the desert didn't let her in but she wouldn't have wanted them to anyway. These people live like animals, she told me. She cooked and cleaned and mended all day. She was in love with Ali. Still she complained. She was happier up north but the visit wouldn't last. She couldn't live without Ali around but the village where he worked was a severe trial for her. The tea was hot. It was hard to hold the glass. I was thinking in the lantern light of the muezzin. He was a short fat man. They had a platform for him. It wasn't tall. He climbed up the few steps and stood inside the little hut and belted out the call. You wouldn't think anyone would hear him, but some of them did and the ones who didn't knew what time it was anyway. People prayed in that country like crazy—as much as five times a day. For some of them, it didn't even matter what was going on. When it was time to pray, they dropped everything and prayed. You could walk into a shop and find the shopkeeper kneeling behind the counter with his head on the ground, praying. The whole village was a small bit of scatter. It might have been a place before the country grew up around it. But now it was a corner of no place in particular thrown away a couple of kilometers off the freeway. The muezzin's platform was the same in the village. It defied all notions of centrality. It was tossed in a corner. You might miss it completely but there it was, little steps with a hut on top. When the muezzin climbed up there to call, he really belted it out. But his voice didn't make it everywhere. It didn't even make a big circle. Instead it fell short and long irregularly in all directions. It flopped here and there between the houses like ropes of rags in the dust. When it was time for me to go, Ali took me to the bus station on a borrowed motorcycle. It was in the morning. I knew when I got off, it would be the last time I would see him. I shook his hand. That place was a place I wasn't going to go back to, I knew. And I was right.

It's funny, I thought, looking at the brown world gridded with roads. I used to pray as a child but at some point I stopped but I don't remember stopping. Lillian taught us to pray when we were small and then she made us go to church. But after a while she stopped. I think she stopped because she didn't like nuns. She got to know some nuns as a child. Those nuns were real bitches—Sister St. Agnes in particular. She would damn a child to hell at the drop of a hat. She damned Lillian to hell for standing out of line, and she damned her to hell for coming back late from the bathroom. Lillian hated the nuns and maybe she hated the whole racket but she taught us to pray and made us go to church anyway. Later, she said it was her mother who made her. It's hard for me to imagine Lillian's mother making anyone do anything. She's so soft and quiet. She's hardly even there. I always thought she was going to die at any minute and when she died it would be soft and quiet like blowing the seeds off a dandelion clock. Nonetheless—according to Lillian—Lillian's mother made her do all sorts of things including teaching us to pray and making us go to church. But then Lillian got sick of her and we didn't have to go anymore. It might have been around that time that I stopped praying. I stopped praying for a long time and then I started up again briefly. I was just out of school. I started praying because I didn't want that girl, the one I could not believe, to be pregnant. If she had a baby, it would be my baby. If she had an abortion, it would be my abortion. I didn't want an abortion but I didn't want a baby on my hands either. I thought if I had a baby on my hands, I'd have this girl on my hands as well. The idea of having this girl on my hands and a baby on my hands was unbearable. So, I prayed. I didn't feel I was being unreasonable. Sex with this girl should have been impossible and her getting pregnant was completely out of the question. As it turned out, we were *thrown together*. We were thrown together again and again. She didn't tell me until she knew. There was no point in praying anymore but I did anyway. I prayed after the fact. I paid when she had herself scraped out. Her body had been scraped out quite a bit when she was a child with cancer. In fact, that's why we thought she couldn't get pregnant. Getting pregnant with her was something of a miracle, in a medical sense. Nonetheless there she was getting scraped out

33

again. Of course, I didn't think of it that way because I never believed a word she said. I stood outside on the sidewalk and watched the women go in and come out, smoking like crazy. The whole thing felt like a car accident. It was all over before any part of it seemed possible, I thought, looking down at the brown world gridded with roads.

It's extremely unlikely that Ray will die falling off of a horse, I thought, looking down at the brown world gridded with roads. It's true, left to his own devices, Ray would be as likely to die falling off a horse as anyone else, maybe more so. But as it is, Lillian won't let him. She lives in terror of accidents. When I was a boy, we visited the farm and Ray got on a horse. There he was cantering around in front of a barn. Lillian made him get off; she didn't want him to break his neck. In fact, she walked right up and pulled him off. When she pulled him off, it looked like she was going to break his neck for him. Her father was a drunk, but he didn't fall off a horse. He had a heart attack in someone's living room not long after Lillian married Ray. Heart attacks don't happen on purpose but at the same time you can hardly call one an accident. Lillian's mother won't visit the grave. Not long after his death, she married someone else, who made bicycles. We all assume Lillian's mother won't visit Lillian's father's grave because he was a drunk. His whole married life he was a drunk. But who knows? There might have been something else. Nancy also lives in terror of accidents, and she suffers for it. When I went to work and we had a yard, I often came home to find her trailing after the girls in the yard with the intention of intervening in the event of an accident. She suffers through all kinds of accidents that haven't even taken place yet, most of which, in fact, never do take place. Though I have nothing to say against safety, I find her concern excessive. I think it's a psychological mechanism. I think somewhere in there, she figures it's better to suffer through an accident in your head than in reality. I think somewhere in there, she figures, if you suffer enough in your head, you won't have to suffer in reality. I think somewhere in there, she figures suffering an accident in your head *prevents* you from having to suffer through it in reality. But when an accident does actually happen, it doesn't help at all. She suffers as much as anyone else, if not more so. She certainly suffered when Lulu broke her arm. She broke her arm falling from the monkey bars. They were the kind you traverse by swinging hand over hand. There Lulu was way up there swinging. They were far too high for her but she had learned to do it all by herself. All summer she had worked and worked on doing it all by herself. I didn't stand under her anymore. All summer I had stood under her but I stopped because she had learned how to do it by herself. In any case, I had left the playground to get cigarettes. A friend was watching from a bench. I saw her from the steps on my way back. I saw her way up there swinging from bar to bar all by herself. Then she fell and when she hit the ground, she started screaming. Her arm was broken in two places just above the elbow. It must have hurt. Nancy suffered for two days until the arm was set and the cast had dried, and she kept suffering afterwards. It's been years now but it wouldn't surprise me if somewhere in there Nancy still suffers, now and again, from the time Lulu broke her arm. I've pretty much put it behind me, and as for Lulu, I have no doubt, she'd break her arm again if we let her, I thought looking down on the brown world gridded with roads.

Kids are resilient, I thought, looking down on the brown world gridded with roads. Unlike adults, kids can put up with a lot. The kind of thing that would destroy an adult never destroys a kid. Or maybe it does destroy them, but it destroys them later when they are adults. Unlike children, adults are, more or less, defenseless. Your average adult is destroyed on a daily basis. They can't help it. They are completely without recourse. It might be the smallest thing, but for adults that doesn't matter. Every straw is the last straw, for adults. Adults are destroyed not only by what happens to them as adults but also by everything that happened to them as children but that they put off. You can only put things off for so long and the time for putting things off gets shorter and shorter the longer you do it. Pretty soon, putting it off is completely out of the question. That's when you know you are an adult. The last time I saw Ray and Lillian, I kicked myself out of the house. We had had an argument. It had to do with their old house. I had let some strangers into Ray and Lillian's old house on Thanksgiving. It might not sound like a big deal, but that house is more than a house to Lillian. Ray and Lillian had been far away visiting someone. A couple of Nancy's friends came to visit us in our apartment with their baby. We made a turkey and everything. We did it for the kids. Kids love holidays. Even babies love holidays. They can tell when the day is a holiday and they love it every time. The man couldn't sleep on our floor because of his back. He carried boxes for a living and it fucked up his back. The couch was too short. Lulu slept with us or she didn't sleep at all. I let them stay at my parent's house. I had the keys. Ray and Lillian weren't around. We had the keys so we could watch the house. They told us to watch the house. They were visiting someone. Later at Christmas, they found out. The neighbors told them. The neighbors were watching the house too. When Ray and Lillian go away, the neighbors always watch the house. When they go, they always tell the neighbors, Watch the house. We watched the house too. I had the keys. It was around Christmas when the neighbors called to tell Ray and Lillian about Nancy's friends staying in their house. Nancy and I and the girls were staying with Ray and Lillian in the little house in the desert. The other house was already on its way out. They were getting rid of it so they could live in the desert. Ray was done working. Now he was going to live in the desert, and Lillian was going with him. We were on the way to a desert too, but one that was halfway around the world. Before we did, we stayed with them. It saved a months' rent on a new lease, and Ray and Lillian wanted to see the girls and it was Christmas. They were crazy about the girls then and still are. It had been a tense visit, but no one had blown up and we only had one night to go before we headed out to the other side of the world. Ray and Lillian wanted to see the girls before we took them away forever. Two nights before we were to leave the neighbors had called to tell Ray and Lillian that I had let someone stay in their house the previous Thanksgiving. That really got under Lillian's skin. Someone was sleeping in her bed, she thought. Someone was fingering her things, she thought. She thought Nancy's friends had spent the entire night in her house wandering from room to room fingering everything they could get their hands on. Nancy's friends were people they didn't know. That was the kicker. For Lillian, having someone she didn't know in her house when she wasn't there was like being raped. Or maybe she was bluffing. In any case, it upset her. It was more than a house to her. Lillian kept it to herself for a day but then decided to let us have it. She let us know we were caught and demanded an apology. The apology was her way of pushing our faces in it. We couldn't keep our guests, you see. In any case, I didn't apologize. Instead, I pushed her face in it. The house was more than a house to her. I pushed her face in that. I didn't like pushing her face in it. But I needed to push something and her face was right there. I liked pushing her face in it. It was a relief. I thought I was kicking myself out and in that way kicking Lillian out. I liked it when I was doing it but felt bad afterwards. I thought I was kicking myself out but, as it turned out, I hadn't kicked anyone out. Everyone was still in. As it turned out, I hated

37

Lillian less than I hated the idea of hating Lillian. So eventually, I shut up and we stayed the night. Ray kept his mouth shut the whole time and he kept his head. He's very cool headed. At that point, you could say just about anything to Ray and he'd keep his head. We could only push him over the brink when we were children. When I was a child I pushed him over the brink on a regular basis but he never hit me. He'd lose his head but get it back before he could hit me. I was quick. I knew Ray was going to lose his head when he said, Holier than thou. As soon as he said, Holier than thou, I knew he was going to lose his head and come after me. I knew he was going to lose his head before *he* did. He never hit me because he always regained his composure before he could hit me. He was cool headed. In this case, he shut up until everyone calmed down and we made it through the night. In the morning, everything was over and Lillian was destroyed. She was standing there in the vestibule looking at the floor, and you could tell just by looking at her that she had been destroyed. She'd been destroyed a hundred times over, but there she was being destroyed again. As for me, standing there in the vestibule, I thought, I'll never go back to that house where the ruckus happened. But here I was on my way there, I thought looking down at the brown world gridded with roads. Then I sat back, pulled the sleeping mask down over my eyes and tried to sleep.

Not long after I left the tree that day I was walking to the mountains, I met this man, I recalled, with the sleeping mask pulled down over my eyes. At first he was a white speck against the orange. As I drew closer, I could see that he was a man. He was standing in front of a house—a mud box with a mud wall enclosing a courtyard in front and a garden in back. It was a small place but he didn't live with the animals. He kept the goat and donkey outside. We exchanged greetings. The greetings were lengthy and involved. In turn, we each affirmed the well being of ourselves, our families, our relatives, the country and the world at large. When it could go on no further, he invited me in for tea. There was fire in his house and a kettle stuffed with mint and short glasses. We sat down. He unwrapped a cone of sugar, chiseled a piece off with a tool made for that purpose, lifted the lid of the kettle with the tool and dropped the sugar in. We waited. He poured out the tea. It was hot and sweet. We exchanged meager news. We drank the tea. He was alone out there. That is, he was alone with his family. They must have been girls. Girls are a curse for those people. Or rather, they are a blessing but only if there are boys around. If there are boys around, sure, girls are a blessing. But if there are no boys, then the girls are a curse. A household of girls with no boys is a curse. They stayed in back. The family lived alone. I had an idea about how this had happened. There must've been a dispute. There must've been a series of disputes. This was a *ksar*—a kind of communal dwelling made of mud. That country was chock full of *ksars*. There was only one family in this one, but it was *ksar* nonetheless. The *ksars* back near the town were huge. They looked like enormous sand castles—people-sized sand castles. People lived in them. Inside, there were no doors. They kept the men and the women separate, but there were no doors. A whole town could live in a *ksar* without doors inside. If a serious dispute arose, you couldn't just shut your door; someone had to leave. Half the people in the *ksar* might leave and build their own *ksar* a hundred yards away. This didn't resolve the dispute. It just cut it off before things could get ugly. If there was a dispute in that *ksar*, half would again have to leave. My idea was that this man's *ksar* came at the end of a long series of disputes. There was a chain of *ksars* each smaller than the previous one stretching all the way from a town-sized *ksar* god-knows-where to this one mud hut out on the plain. Each *ksar* in the chain harbored an

39

unresolved dispute like a broken rib. The sting of these disputes increased as the disputes themselves became more and more recent. Here, at the end, the sting was fresh and agonizing. This man's family could live only with themselves. And so they did. Here. The women must've been in back. They were silent. The donkey outside with the goat cried piteously. The man went out and hit it with a stick. It kept groaning and crying. I finished my tea. The man came back. We blessed each other. I blessed his staying. He blessed my going. I left.

Buddy, we're here, said the man next to me, nudging me awake. I pushed the mask up. The man was leaning across my body pointing out the window. I looked out.

There it was, the city, laid out beneath me, with its white towers and tangled highways. It was laid out just like it had been there all along. We would land soon, and when we landed, I would be in the middle of it. The city would be the whole world then and the idea of flying over it completely out of the question. Cities are like that. When you are in the middle of a city, the city feels like the whole world.

You must be starving, the man next to me said, settling back into his seat. You haven't eaten a damn thing. I've been eating everything for you. I'm not crazy about airplane food, the man said. But something about being on an airplane makes me hungry. Airplane food doesn't go down well. I'll suffer for all this airplane food I've eaten. I'll suffer all morning, but I can't help myself. When I get on an airplane, I get hungry like there's no tomorrow. It was nice of you to give me your tray, the man said. Are you a vegetarian or something? I'm not a vegetarian though I can see the sense in it. Health-wise, I mean. I like meat. Red meat especially. I could live off hamburgers. I practically do live off hamburgers when I'm on the ground, that is. You can't get a good hamburger on a plane to save your life. Everything is microwaved. As soon as I get on the ground, I'm going to head over to the first hamburger joint I can find and have a hamburger. I'm famished. Here I've eaten twice as much as I had any right to expect (thanks to you, buddy) but I still can't wait to hit the ground and find a hamburger. Do you know of any good hamburger places down there? I've never been down there myself. That is to say, this is my first time. I wouldn't be going there now except my client moved. My client moved to the city down there, so if I want to talk to my client I have to go down there too. No point in going to the other city where my client used to live. He was the only client I had there, so when he moved, he took that city right off the map, as far as I'm concerned. In my business you fly a lot. I'll bet I spend almost as much time up here in the air as down there on the ground. Not too many people can say that. Pilots, I suppose, spend a lot of time in the air. But I can tell you, when I go back it will be with a different pilot. I don't think they work them that hard—on account of accidents. Planes would be falling out of the sky left and right. Fatigue, you know. Those pilots wouldn't be able keep their eyes open. Of course there are pills for that, but you wouldn't want your pilot taking pills, would you? No, our pilot will be hanging around a cocktail bar some place, when I'm climbing back up into this airplane. I don't take any pills, and I can sleep just like a baby because I don't have to fly the plane. It's in my blood. I bet I could sleep standing up if I had to. I could sleep standing up with my eyes wide open. In fact, I have whole days like that. I'm standing up, but I'm so dead tired—asleep actually—that I don't have a clue what's going on. I might not hear a word you say even if you were standing right in front of me. That's why I carry this around.

The man pulled a tiny tape recorder of his suit pocket and showed it to me on the palm of his hand.

With this little baby, the man went on, you could talk to me for an hour and I wouldn't miss a thing even if I wasn't listening to a word you were saying. This little baby picks it all up for me so I can listen later when I'm back at my hotel. I carry it everywhere I go. I carry it right here in my suit. Voice activated. I don't even have to turn it on. Now suppose you said something... Go ahead, say something, said the man. Sure anything, said the man. Say something. It wont' work unless you say something, said the man. Go ahead, anything. Just la la la is OK. Aw come on, said the man. Just say something. OK, I'll do it. Just point it at me like this. No at *me*. So the mike is pointed...yeah that's right. **La**! the man said. You see, there it goes! the man said. You can feel the little motor whirring, can't you? It kinda tickles, doesn't it? That baby just woke right up the moment it heard my voice. O.K., I'll take it back now. No point in wasting—

After that, there was just a humming noise and then the tape ran out with a click. I turned off the machine and put it back into the little fridge next to the mirror. I took out some ice and a little bottle of Scotch and made myself a drink in a plastic cup. I took it out to the balcony with me and lit a cigarette. The lights were still on around the pool. They must leave them on all night, I thought, looking down on the blue water. It's far too late for a swim. Everyone is fast asleep.

I bet people hardly ever swim in that pool, I thought looking down on the blue water in the pool. This is not that kind of a hotel. People come to this hotel to sleep not to swim in pools. They probably don't even know there's a pool back here until after they're checked in. I didn't know. As far as this hotel goes, out in the middle of nowhere as it is, that pool is just an ornament. The people who made the hotel probably just put a pool there because they thought hotels ought to have pools. Hotels with pools command higher rates, they might have thought. Maybe they anticipated arguments with disgruntled customers in which the disgruntled customer complained about the rates. You charge that rate, a disgruntled customer might have said, and you don't even have a pool? Customers would say that whether they wanted to use a pool or not. The people who made the hotel knew. That's why they put in the pool. They could charge whatever they wanted regardless. There's no other hotel for miles around. If you are driving around in this corner of nowhere, and you have to stop, you have to stop here. If you stop here, you have to pay the rate. You have to pay the rate whether you use the pool or not. What's more if you complain about the rate, the hotel owners can always point to the pool. But we have a pool! they might say. What do you expect? You're paying for the pool whether you use it or not. Of course it's good for kids. Kids love pools. They don't care if they've been stuck in a car all day driving through miles and miles of nowhere. It doesn't matter how late you arrive here at the one and only hotel. It doesn't matter how exhausted they might be. Kids love pools, and they're going to want to jump right in. Pools are like holidays for kids. It doesn't matter when you encounter one or what else is going on, as soon as those kids see the pool, it's a big holiday for them. They jump right in. Of course that drives the rates up. The liability, I mean. It pushes the insurance rates right up, and the insurance rates push the hotel

43

rates right up. If a kid drowns, it's the hotel that is liable even if there's a fence and a sign that says, Swim at Your Own Risk or something to that effect. It won't matter one iota to a jury if there's a drowned kid involved, especially if there's insurance. The insurance company will pay because the parents will make them, if they can stand it. If they can stand it, the parents will make the insurance company pay as exorbitant a sum as possible. Who wouldn't? Of course, they might not be able to stand it. If their kid drowned in a pool, the parents might be utterly destroyed. They might be so destroyed that pursuing a settlement is completely out of the question. They might not want to have anything more to do with it. The very idea of a settlement might appear so irrelevant as to be insulting, to the destroyed parents. A destroyed parent might not be able to think about money. The destroyed parents are thinking about their drowned child. There's nothing further from money than a drowned child. Drowned children are as far from money as it is possible to get. The idea that the drowned child could in some way be equivalent to an exorbitant sum of money might be completely beyond the ken of the destroyed parent. The idea that the drowned child could actually be transformed into an exorbitant sum of money might strike the destroyed parents as satanically perverse. The destroyed parents know they are in Hell; they hardly need the transformation of their drowned child, with limbs etc… into a big crate of fresh green dollar bills to confirm that fact. Who would? On the other hand, the destroyed parent might be unable to think of anything but money. After all, the destroyed parent has nothing. It's hard to think about a drowned child as a positive quantity. The destroyed parent has less than nothing. In that case, pursuing a settlement makes about as much sense as pursuing anything else. In that instance, the destroyed parent will fight tooth and nail for a settlement. The destroyed parent will pursue a settlement with monomaniacal zeal. After all, what else is there? There is no child. There is something less than a child. There's nothing left but the settlement. The destroyed parent, emptied completely—more than emptied—by the drowning of the child—will become possessed and though obtaining an exorbitant settlement will not make the slightest difference, you can bet the destroyed parent will be unable to rest before obtaining one. And you can bet they will obtain a settlement, a large settlement, the largest they could imagine or even larger than they could have imagined—and they will be able to rest, at last, in Hell, I thought, looking down at the blue water in the pool.

Lillian once told me about this guy whose daughter drowned in a pool, I recalled, looking down at the blue water in the pool. He thought she was asleep. He was reading a book somewhere. He put his daughter down for a nap and then went off to read a book. He thought his daughter was asleep but instead she was awake. She got right out of bed and wandered off to drown herself in the pool. She was a small child. Falling in and whatever thrashing around she did hardly made a splash. She did that while this guy was reading his book. He didn't have a clue. He thought she was sleeping. He thought she was sleeping right up until he wandered up by the pool and found her there face down in the water. For a second or two, he probably still thought she was sleeping even then. But the crazy part was, Lillian told me, the book he was reading was all about this guy whose daughter got drowned in a pool. Can you imagine that? Lillian asked. What are the chances?

The girls are safe, I thought looking down at the blue water in the pool. Right now, the girls are safe at school. Nancy is at work, and the tortoises are crawling around in their tray in the empty apartment. Here I am on the other side of the world at the only hotel in the middle of nowhere. Ray and Lillian are in their little house at the end of the highway that runs to the foot of the mountains. They're waiting now. They're waiting for me to show up and hear what Ray has to say. Lillian has made snacks and packed them in the fridge. Carrot sticks, celery sticks, grapes, cubes of watermelon all packed in little plastic boxes stacked on top of each other in the fridge. Ray is watching the news. Except for the snacks, it's an evening like any other at their place. Without the snacks, you would never know they were expecting anyone—least of all me. But nothing is right. Ray is watching the news but he's not watching the news. He's watching the news but he can't follow anything that they are talking about. Pictures are washing down over the screen but none of the pictures makes any sense. It's irritating. It's irritating to be subjected to so continuous a flow of unintelligible information. With every passing minute, Ray's irritation becomes more acute. He won't be able to sit there much longer. As for Lillian, with the snacks done, she has nothing to do with her hands. She's going to sit down with a book, but just like Ray, she won't be able to concentrate. Words from the book are going to come whispering through her head but she won't be able to make out what's going on. The book will be there open on her lap and though she'll be able to read the words, the sense of it will escape her completely. There they are the two of them in that little house at the end of the highway at the foot of the mountains, each becoming more and more distracted with every passing minute. They are waiting for me. They want me to come, but at the same time they are dreading it. There Ray is like a boulder in his chair and there Lillian is, sitting as lightly as a moth, ready to flutter into the air at any given moment—both of them becoming more and more charged with dread with every passing moment. Ray sat down in front of the TV to distract himself from the dread of my approach but it's not working. Instead the dread of my approach is distracting him from the television. The television is useless. The news flows down the screen in an unending wash of images. What's more all the images are of violence. The news is always violence; the preparation for violence, the aftermath of violence or violence itself. The news provides an unending stream of images depicting violence; violence deferred, violence escaped, violence enacted or violence survived. And none of it, in Ray's distracted condition, makes the least amount of sense. Instead of alleviating his anxiety about my inexorable approach, my impending arrival, all these images of violence—rendered unintelligible in Ray's state of extreme distraction—feed his anxiety. The more Ray seeks distraction, the less distracted he becomes. And Lillian, by this time, has left her book to flit about in the kitchen, feeding Ray's distraction and failing to alleviate her own. In fact, she has abandoned the book less to alleviate her own dread than to surrender to it. When I arrive, they both know, I will disrupt. Whether Ray succeeds in imparting to me what he has waited so long to impart, or Lillian succeeds in obstructing my reception of it, there will be a disruption. In fact, it has started already. The very shadow of my approach has already cleaved Ray and Lillian from the intelligibility of their own habits, I thought, sitting in the silent hotel, looking down on the blue water in the pool.

The Scotch was gone. I got up. I walked through the silence of the hotel room to get more from the fridge where another little bottle was wedged between the Dictaphone and the inner white wall. I grabbed some ice. I mixed another drink and returned to the balcony to look down on the blue water of the pool below.

Lulu had asthma when she was a baby, I recalled, looking down at the pool. When she had an attack, we stayed up all night listening to her breathing. It sounded awful. Every breath sounded like a struggle. Every breath sounded as if it would be the last. We listened closely to try to discern if it were getting better or worse. Most of the time it was impossible to tell. We had medicine but it didn't always work and if she got too much, her heart would start racing. You could hear that too. I put my head against her chest and heard her heart racing and then took my head away and I could still hear her heart racing. I could spend all night listening to her struggle for breath with her heart racing. It drove Nancy crazy. She would cry but then eventually she would sleep. When Nancy was asleep, all I wanted was a cigarette. I lay there listening to Lulu struggle for breath with her heart racing and thought about sneaking out for a smoke. It was the anxiety that did it, and being up late. If you smoke, and you are up late filled with anxiety, you are going to want to smoke. It took about ten minutes to ride the elevator down to the street, smoke and ride the elevator back up to where we lived. What could happen in ten minutes? I would think. I was worried about Lulu but I was also worried about Nancy. Nancy usually woke up when I left. Even if I left for just a minute, she woke up. From a dead sleep, the first words out of her mouth were always, *Where were you?* It was a kind of reflex. The waking up was a reflex and the words were a reflex. Sometimes she would ask even before I'd left the room. It made me angry. I thought, here I am lying awake, filled with anxiety, listening to Lulu struggle for breath with her heart racing and all I want is a cigarette, but if I get up, ride the elevator to the street, smoke and come back, the first words out of Nancy's mouth will be, *Where were you?* I could lay awake for hours listening and yearning for a cigarette and getting angrier and angrier all the while. Other times, I went out to smoke regardless of what Nancy would say. If she woke up, we fought bitterly in whispers. But sometimes, she didn't. Other times, Lulu's lips would look blue in the dark and I'd haul her off to the emergency room. The emergency room was always a circus filled with drunks and the victims of violence and asthmatic children—all of them unaccountably bored. Emergencies rooms are permeated with an atmosphere of boredom. Nothing feels less like an emergency than an emergency room. Sometimes Lulu would come out of it right there. Other times she'd still be struggling for breath when the doctors showed up and they'd give her a shot that would have her bouncing around and talking at a hundred miles an hour within minutes. In any case, I was always happy to get back home to Nancy. Coming back home to Nancy with a breathing Lulu was a pleasure and a relief. They'd go to bed together, and I'd sit out in front of the building and smoke. I've spent a lot of time in front of various buildings smoking. Nancy got me to quit for a while but I started up again because I found when I was standing in front of buildings I had nothing to do with my hands, I thought looking down at the blue water in the pool.

Missy gave us much less trouble as a baby, I thought, looking down on the pool. No asthma. She got out a lot and climbed things like a monkey but she never broke her arm. Some people are born lucky. Missy was born lucky I can tell. I was born lucky too. When I was a kid I took all kinds of chances and never got called to account. I got my friends to do the craziest stuff but no one ever broke so much as a finger. My friend's mother said I had nine lives and I believed her. We climbed everything in sight. We spent a lot of time around railroad bridges and deep water and thin ice. I even got them to climb the second highest freestanding TV tower in the world. It happened to be in our town. Our town was like that. Climbing it took hours and when we got to the top, the ground looked like a figment of our imaginations. Fireworks were exploding *beneath* us. It was the fourth of July. There wasn't much room to sit up there but you could hold on to this antenna that shot up right in the middle.

49

Later my friend joined the navy. He spent some time around places where people were killing each other, but he never killed anyone or got killed himself. Now he spends a lot of time in Japan. Later he identified that antenna as a microwave broadcaster. If it had been turned on, we'd all have been fried from the inside out. It happened to sailors occasionally. We hadn't a clue up there. The worst thing that happened to Missy as a baby was when she swallowed a coin. Kids love to put things in their mouths. She came out of our bedroom gagging on blood and vomit. We thought she had the flu. Then she said, I ate money. She was sharp for a toddler. I picked her up and carried her to the hospital. As chance would have it, there was a hospital right next door. This was a rich country. It was the richest place I'd ever lived. It was chock full of hospitals. The hospital next door was an Arab hospital. I must confess the Arab doctors did not enjoy my full confidence. I didn't have full confidence in Arab doctors because they were Arabs. Half the wings of the hospital seemed to be named after terrorist groups and all the beds were pointed towards Mecca. Also, it had been my experience that Arab doctors never explained anything and prescribed too much medicine. Once they gave Nancy so many antibiotics that the inside of her mouth turned black. In this instance, I was glad the hospital was right there. There was no emergency room. Instead the receptionist took me to a doctor who took me to another doctor and so on. I carried Missy all over that hospital running from doctor to doctor. They couldn't get the coin out with their hands. They did an X-ray. The X-ray had the coin perched between the tube to her lungs and the one to her stomach. I followed this veiled woman all over the hospital. We rode around in the elevators. I ended up in the basement in an abandoned little room with Missy still in my arms, choking. The woman left us there. Then some doctors came in and took Missy away behind some swinging doors. I wasn't allowed in. I don't know how long I stood there. It was dead quiet. There wasn't a soul around. There was no place to sit except behind a tiny desk with a magazine open across the top. The magazine was open to a full-page spread of shiny medical equipment. I couldn't read the script. It was familiar to me. I had been surrounded by that script for years, but still I couldn't read it. I spent quite some time in that little room looking at the familiar script I couldn't read. Eventually someone came and got me. As it turned out, the doctors had put a tool down Missy's throat to pull the coin out but instead it slipped into her stomach. Nancy stayed with her in the hospital that night. The coin came out of Missy's butt the next day. The nurse saved it for us in a little plastic bottle. Around noon, she said it was safe to go home but we could stay longer if we wanted to.

I hate hospitals, I thought, looking down on the blue water in the pool. I hate being in a hospital myself, and I hate visiting people in hospitals. If you are visiting someone in a hospital, you have to hang around someone who is sick or dying. If you are not visiting in a hospital, you yourself are either sick or dying. Lots of people die in hospitals. It's mostly what hospitals are for. If someone doesn't die on his first trip to a hospital, he'll die on his second. If he doesn't die on the second trip, it will be the third. In any case, he'll die on the last trip. In fact, they'll take him there for that very reason. So far, I've only stayed in a hospital once myself. It was when I was a kid. I had broken my head. It was the result of stupidity pure and simple. My friend's mother had bought something. It came in a long narrow box. I can't remember what she bought. In fact I can't remember anything about this particular accident. I broke my head after all. So the game was someone walked around in the long narrow box and everyone else wailed on the box with sticks. When it was my turn in the box, I tripped over something on the

51

sidewalk and hit the pavement like a tree falling. The side of my head slapped against the sidewalk and cracked up all around the ear. My friends couldn't figure out why I didn't get out of the box and tried tickling. Eventually, they got Lillian who hauled me off to the hospital. I was unconscious for a couple of days. I don't remember any of that. I only remember rolling around the hospital in a wheel chair at a hundred miles an hour. My friend was pushing. I don't know if I ever knew this particular friend or not, but I knew he was my friend. He hadn't even been at the accident but he came to visit me at the hospital every day. He visited and pushed me down the long hallways at a hundred miles an hour every afternoon. As it turned out, this particular hospital was a lot of fun. There didn't seem to be anyone else there. This friend of mine disappeared later. Most people disappear sooner or later, but this friend of mine really disappeared. That is, people looked for him. Eventually I found his name and sent letters to that name but no one ever wrote back. Both his parents were alive last I heard, but they broke up shortly before my friend disappeared. They broke up because they were both highly intelligent and tortured each other. His father had been in a war. In the war, he flew in airplanes. Afterwards, he became a psychiatrist. But he still had this parachute. It was for trunks and boxes. He took us out with it once. We went to the park on a windy day and let the parachute drag us around the turf. That was a lot of fun and as far as I can remember we didn't ruin the parachute. But his dad never took it out again. It was only for that one day.

I woke up in the chair with the Scotch in my lap. I went in and took off my clothes then crawled in between the cold clean hotel sheets. I felt a little funny. My knee was still bleeding like crazy. It was sure to make a mess, but what could I do? I crawled in and waited for sleep. But sleep wasn't coming. No way. Not tonight,

I thought. Sleep is completely impossible tonight, I thought. There are nights when you lay yourself down between cold clean hotel sheets and you know immediately that sleep is completely impossible. This is one of those nights, I thought. I was drinking Scotch, I thought, but I may as well have been drinking coffee. Scotch puts Ray to sleep, but it keeps me awake. It puts me to sleep first but then it keeps me awake. It puts me to sleep for a short time and then keeps me awake all night. If I drink too much, it fills me with nausea. I can spend all night wide-awake and filled with nausea from having drunk too much Scotch. You would think I'd stop drinking it but I never do. I keep drinking it because every time I think it's going to put me to sleep. It never does. Nonetheless every time I find myself awake after everyone else has gone to bed and the night has grown quiet, if there's Scotch around, I drink it. I drink it to help me sleep. Scotch puts Ray to sleep. It puts him to sleep right in front of the TV. Later, Lillian gets him up to go to bed and he gets up and he walks up the stairs, but even up and walking, Ray is asleep. It's the Scotch that does it. Even now, I thought looking at the ceiling as I lay between the cold clean hotel sheets on the bed, Ray is undoubtedly fast asleep in their little house at the foot of the mountains, but I'm wide awake here in this hotel room in the middle of nowhere. In both cases, it's the Scotch that did it. Lillian's father was a drunk and Nancy's father was a drunk but Ray is not a drunk and neither am I. How could he be? You can't be a drunk if you fall asleep after two or three drinks. It's impossible. Similarly I can't be a drunk because Scotch inevitably fills me with nausea. I suppose Ray could be a drunk but you'd never know it because he would be sleeping. He'd be a sleeping drunk. Of course being a sleeping drunk is almost the same as not being a drunk at all. I too could be a drunk, I suppose, if I could master my nausea. But I can't. I can't even come close. When it comes to nausea, I am completely without defenses. I can't master my nausea because my nausea inevitably masters me. It masters me instantly and completely. I can't do anything when I'm nauseated—not even be a drunk; not even sleep.

Right now, I thought, looking at the ceiling as I lay between the cold clean hotel sheets, half the world is filled with sleeping people, and on the other half all the people are awake. Here I am in the sleeping part of the world but I'm wide-awake. Nancy and the girls are over on the waking part of the world and they are also wide-awake but so is everyone else (over there). This half of the world, the sleeping half, I thought, is dotted all over with insomniacs winking among the dark mass of sleeping people. Everywhere we look—we insomniacs—we see sleeping people. We can't see each other. The dark mass of sleeping people gets in the way. We know we are awake because everyone else is asleep. Lillian, for example, is wide-awake and utterly still out on the porch with a book on her lap surrounded by encroaching darkness. And here I am wide-awake between the cold clean sheets on the hotel bed. But we can't see each other. Insomnia is a profoundly isolating experience, I thought, looking at the ceiling. Nancy gets insomnia, and I get insomnia but we never have insomnia at the same time. Simultaneous insomnia is unthinkable. Sometimes Nancy can't sleep because she worries. Sometimes I can't sleep because I've drunk too much Scotch. When I can't sleep, I go to the living room. When Nancy can't sleep, she goes to the kids' room. On the exceedingly rare occasions when both Nancy and I can't sleep at the same time, we never stay awake together. Insomnia is a solitary pursuit. The whole point of insomnia is to be awake and surrounded by sleeping people. If I can't sleep because I've drunk too much Scotch and at the same time Nancy can't sleep because she is worrying, inevitably we stay awake separately. Nancy leaves the bed to go to my children's room to be surrounded by sleeping

54

children, and I leave the bed to go to the living room to look out the giant windows at the sleeping city sprawled below me on three sides. Insomniacs repel each other like the like poles of magnets. In the instances when we both have insomnia and separate, even our big bed is left alone in the big bedroom with the blanket thrown halfway open. Even the big bed is wide-awake, I thought, looking up at the ceiling from between the cold clean sheets on the hotel bed. Suddenly I felt like I was getting sick.

I hate being sick, I thought, feeling sick between the cold clean sheets on the hotel bed. But at least there's no one around. Being sick by yourself is awful, but being sick around other people is a hundred times worse. When I'm sick at home, I thought, I always try to disappear. I close the door, crawl into bed, pull the blanket over my head and wait. I tell everyone, I'll come out when I'm well. And I do. I stay in with the door shut until I feel better and then I come out and jump right back into things *as if I had never been sick.* I don't like other people being around me when I'm sick because I know they want to get away. No one likes being around a sick person, not even the sick person himself. I don't like being around sick people. When I'm around a sick person, my first impulse is to get away. When I'm sick, I'm sure the people unfortunate enough to be around me—a sick person—want to get away too. And in general, they do. The people who can get away, do get away. Why not? What's to keep them there? You may find yourself sick and surrounded by a whole group of people who want to get away. You may be thinking, being sick is bad but it's even worse being sick around all these people who really want to get away. Don't worry! The people who can get away will get away soon enough. They'll get away lickety-split. There's always a reason to get away, or if there's no reason at the moment, one will surely come along.

One minute you are surrounded, even smothered, by people who want to get away and the next, you are all by yourself—if you're lucky. But more often than not, there will be people left over. These are the people who want to get away but can't. These people can't get away because they feel they really ought to stay. They want to get away but they've mastered that impulse—the impulse to get away—and replaced it with the compulsion to stay. So instead of getting away, what they really want to do, they stay and the more they want to get away, the more they find themselves compelled to stay. The people who are truly repulsed by illness—repulsed to the degree that this repulsion could almost be considered an illness itself, a morbid repulsion—nine times out of ten are the very same people who, confronted with an illness, will go way out of their way to stay. You can't get rid of them, and you know the whole time they are sitting there, locked in place beside your bed, their dearest wish is to get away, far away, as far away as possible from this illness that repulses them. These people *can't* get away. These people are trapped. These people—the people who want to get away but can't—are utterly dependent on you, the sick person, to let them off the hook, but the only way you can let them off the hook is to bring the whole matter to some conclusion. They sit by your bedside with every mental fiber drawn toward the hope of some conclusion and, at that point, it won't matter which. They might hope one moment that you get better and the next that you die or conversely hope you die one moment and that you get better the next or possibly hope for both at the same time—that you get better and die simultaneously. For a long time, it won't matter which. But if things go on long enough, these people will be wishing singularly and fervently for your death. At that point, your death is better, for them, than your getting better because death is more decisive. Anyone can get better and then the very next moment get worse again.

Getting better is a kind of tease. No one gets better permanently. Getting better is a kind of lull in the progress of getting worse. It's a lull and, in that way, a prolongation. It's a prolongation of an intolerable situation. At that point, these people want you to die because at that point, your death is their only way out. Your death has become their release, I thought, feeling like I might be sick, looking up at the ceiling between the cold clean sheets of the hotel bed.

Suddenly I remembered Mou. He lived in the town in that hot country with me and Ali and the moulay. I had thought there were three of us, but actually there were four, I recalled, looking up at the ceiling, feeling like I might be sick. He was a bit different because he was from there. That made him different. I didn't know Mou until Mou and Mr. Tagine took me to Mou's village to meet his mother and look at the children. The skinny moulay wouldn't come along. He was a moulay and from a big city—from a big city going way, way back. Those people are like animals, he thought though he never said it. Mr. Tagine was a whole nother kettle of fish, as they say. He didn't really count. His name meant "stew." That was a real riot for him. Mr. Stew. Mou thought Mr. Tagine was an idiot. Mr. Tagine thought Mou was an out and out communist and would have drunk the blood of the ruling classes if he could have, and he was absolutely right. Mou would have lined them all up against a wall if he could have. But he knew he couldn't. Mou knew it just wasn't in the cards, but he thought it just wasn't in the cards *for now*. He thought just maybe it would be in the cards in the future, and when that happened, he would be ready. Meanwhile, to bide his time, he practiced ethnology on his own people. He wrote down everything they did because he knew they would soon disappear. His village was vestigial, he thought. It couldn't last much longer. In fact, it was dead. He walked around the village like he was walking around a museum. He wanted it to be gone as much as anyone else, but he didn't want it to disappear without a trace. He wanted a record because his village was also an indictment. The way his people lived was an indictment against the comfortable world. He hated the whole situation, but he wrote it down so people would know. He wanted the people in the comfortable world to know that his people had lived like this. They would never believe it. But he wanted them to know anyway, and he wanted them to know it was their fault. He had translated some songs for me. They were the songs his people sang when they were doing backbreaking labor. Subsistence agriculture is no picnic. It's really hard, and it doesn't always work. That is to say, you can break your back all year long and still not subsist. Most of the songs were about how hard the villagers were working and the villager's landlords—damning them to Hell. Mou also played the *oud*. He was folklore all over. So we took a truck over to his village to look at the children and meet his mother. His father was dead, but a bunch of other male relatives were still around. His mother ate with her hands. She called forks and spoons the devil's fingers. Everyone in that village ate with their hands. There wasn't a single fork or spoon in the whole place. The children scared the shit out of me. There were a lot of them, and they had a tendency to swarm. But it might have been the flies. There were flies everywhere. The people lived with the animals and everything was covered with flies. The flies were maddening. They put me in a state. I hate flies. I couldn't think about anything else. All I could think about was the flies. The children might not have been so scary if it hadn't been for the flies. The children looked like they could eat you alive. They had a tendency to swarm and touch. Who doesn't like the touch of a child? But if there are a lot of children, swarms of children, it's different. They were hungry, and they were active. Hunger hadn't dulled these children.

58

Hunger had sharpened these children. They were sharp and active and you could see a sharp, active hunger in their eyes. These children, I thought, would eat me alive if they could. The flies were making me nuts. Mou said Germans came through in busses and threw candy out the window. It had ruined them, Mou said. It turned them into beggars, so now every time they saw a white face they swarmed. Mr. Tagine thought the whole situation was hilarious. His village wasn't much different but there was a bit more food there and the animals stayed outside. Without Mou, I thought, these children would eat me alive. A sharp word from Mou scattered them instantly. But as soon as he stepped away—to talk to someone, to talk about something secret, or maybe just to say goodbye to his mother—the children came back. They thought I had candy. I didn't bring any but even if I had there would never have been enough. If I had brought candy, I wouldn't have let on. I wouldn't have wanted them to know about it. I wouldn't have wanted them even to smell it. You could tell just looking into their sharp, hungry faces that the whiff of candy would throw them right over the brink. They were sticking their hands in my pockets when the truck came.

I rolled out of the bed, crawled to the bathroom and threw up. I felt much better. I rested there by the toilet feeling much better. Then I turned on the light, brushed my teeth, washed out my mouth, turned off the light and walked back through the silence of the hotel room and crawled back into bed. When I looked up, the ceiling wasn't there anymore, just the sky.

There were some girls in that poor country too, I recalled, looking at the sky, two of them. They lived together in a little house. It was in the mountains in the north where it was beautiful and cold. They had snow. They had trees and rocks

59

with water running over them, cutting through the snow. In their little house, I drank tea with them—all of us wrapped up in blankets in the cold morning. It was very cozy. The two of them were managing an orphanage. They had volunteered for this job, but as it turned out, they were in way over their heads. There were too many babies and not enough of anything else. There weren't enough dryers, for example. You could hang out the blankets, but they didn't dry fast enough. The babies slept in wet blankets and it was cold. They got sick and then they died. A couple died every so often. The girls buried them. There was no one else to do it. They were orphans after all. Those girls were in way over their heads. It should have destroyed them. Maybe it had destroyed them but they wouldn't know that until they were adults. They had a grave, tired, hollowed out look but they weren't destroyed. Or if they were, they didn't know it. They had volunteered for the orphanage. They hadn't volunteered to bury babies. Who would volunteer for that? It was, as it turned out, part of the job. The girls had learned a lot in school. They learned about orphans and orphanages and what to do with orphans and orphanages. There were too many babies and not enough help and not enough dryers. Even without the wet bedding, some of those babies would have died. The babies weren't in great shape to begin with. Some of them were deaf; others were blind; others were infected. They all had problems. In most cases, it had something to do with the way they were born. You can bet they weren't born in hospitals. There were no hospitals for miles around but even if there had been one, those babies wouldn't have been born there. They were born on the sly. An unwanted pregnancy was a very sticky situation in that place. The mother of an unwanted baby could get her legs broken. Her own brothers would do it. It was a matter of honor. So you can bet when those unwanted babies were born, there was no doctor around or midwife or anyone else. Those babies were born in the dark and all alone with their terrified mothers. They were born in the woods somewhere, in the snow, and then their terrified mothers brought them to the orphanage—if they were lucky. Infanticide is a crime. It's a worse crime than having an unwanted baby. But who wants their legs broken? If the mother of the unwanted baby was more afraid of god than she was of her brothers, she'd bring the unwanted baby to the orphanage. Bringing the baby to the orphanage was taking a chance with her brothers, but god saw everything. And you can bet those babies weren't in the best shape when they got there. Not after a birth like that. They had problems. All of them had problems. In a situation like that, some of them would have had to die whether the bedding was wet or dry. You could have had one full-sized dryer for every kid in the place, and babies were still going to die, and the girls would still have to bury them. They were exhausted. They had this tired, grave, hollowed out look. Those girls were, in a word, destroyed, but as yet they hadn't a clue about what had happened to them. It wasn't easy to bury a baby in the snow. The ground wouldn't take them. You had to thaw it out first and even then digging the hole was no picnic. Of course most of them made it. Children are resilient— even babies. Some of the babies died but most of them made it. They made it through the wet blankets. Once they were out of diapers, their chances improved dramatically. If a baby made it out of diapers, its chances—as far as not dying goes—were almost as good as anyone else's. That's not to say from that point on, everything was golden. Babies aren't houseplants. They require a certain amount of human contact. Their brains require it. Those girls couldn't cuddle thirty-five babies. There was never enough help and the help there was didn't understand about brains and human contact. As a result, the ones who made it suffered from a lack of attention. They don't get enough attention, the girls told me. I met a kid there as blank as a sheet of paper. He hadn't

61

gotten enough attention. You couldn't get a rise out of him to save your life. I kept putting a ball in his hand and taking it out again. I was giving him the ball. I said, here you have it; it's yours. Then after a while, I took it away. It was like a game. It missed him completely. You could give it to him and take it away and give it to him and take it away all day long. It was all the same to him.

Lillian is out there now, I thought looking up at the sky. Ray will have drunk enough Scotch to have fallen asleep at this point, and Lillian has taken the book out to the porch to read. When Lillian takes the book out to the porch to read, it means she has reached a point of exhaustion that is as close to actual sleep as it can possibly be without quite reaching it. You might think at that stage, after a while of sitting out there on the porch with the book in lap, sleep would settle on her right out of the dark air. You might think, after a while out there on the porch in the encroaching dark, sleep might settle on Lillian like dew, spreading across her hair and shoulders. You might think you'd find her there in the morning asleep in her chair, her head lolling back, the book askew on her lap. But sleep never does settle on Lillian. Instead age settles on her. It settles like dust. It settles like cobwebs. And with each passing moment, she becomes more and more still and more and more awake. You can tell because her eyes are open. Lillian flits around from the moment she wakes up until the moment Ray loses consciousness in the bedroom. Then she goes out to the porch to read and as she reads all the movement leaks out her. Age settles on her. It settles like dust. It settles like cobwebs. Lillian, out there on the porch in the encroaching darkness, becomes still and more still with every passing moment and at the same time, she becomes more awake; and at the same time, she becomes older. And then after hours of sitting there, at the deepest point in the trough of the night,

Lillian reaches a state of absolute immobility and absolute age with the book on her lap and her eyes wide open. She can stay out all night like that, I thought, looking up at the sky.

I saved a man's life once, I thought looking at the sky. I worked at a pharmacy. I hated it. I didn't mind working. I hated sitting in front of the counter waiting for someone to approach. I could chit-chat with the other guy when he was around, but he wasn't always there and I didn't always have anything to say. I never got to know that guy. We spent hours behind that counter chit-chatting but I never got to know him. When that guy wasn't around, I stole mints out of a little bucket on the counter like crazy. I can still taste those mints. When the other guy was around but we had nothing to say to each other, I used to hide in the basement. There were all these plastic bottles down there in this cage. I liked to sit down there and put the caps on. There was a big box of plastic bottles and next to it a big plastic bag filled with the tops. I could put the tops on the bottles all day long. I didn't mind it. It was less boring than sitting behind the counter because down in the cage in the basement you knew no one was going to approach. You could daydream. You could think. It was down in that basement that I first realized that every other person in the world had a life as vivid as my own. It seemed like a big deal at the time, but it's hard for me to say that it has made any difference. Time passed quickly. God knows what the pharmacists thought I was up to. I think, if I hadn't saved this guy's life, they would have fired me. They would have fired me because I spent so much time in the basement and because I stole mints like a maniac. But they couldn't fire me after I saved this guy's life. I saved his life right in front of their pharmacy after all. It happened like this: This old guy came in for medicine, got it and left. Then there was some kind of ruckus out in front of the shop. A woman came in and asked if anyone knew CPR. As it happened, I had just finished this training course in high school. If it had happened even a week or two later, I don't think I would have done anything. As it was, I was incapable of getting out of it. After all, those were the exact words that began the drill: does anyone know CPR? I was on the spot. I had to do something because to do nothing would have been a lie. I didn't mind lying too much, but in this case, the lie would have been the same as killing this man myself. I didn't want to save the man but I didn't want his death on my hands either. So I said, I know CPR! (just like in the drill), and walked out to save his life ardently hoping he would have recovered before I reached him. I was hoping he would recover before I reached him because I didn't want to have anything to do with it. Besides, I couldn't really remember how to do CPR. It was the numbers that screwed me up. You are supposed to push so many times and count so many times and push so many times and count so many times. That was all I knew. The numbers were completely beyond me. The old guy was lying on his back on the sidewalk twitching like an epileptic. In fact, he was an epileptic. His tongue was stuck in his mouth. His mouth was bleeding and yellow stuff was coming out too. I still don't know what that yellow stuff was. Mostly, I knew, you could leave epileptics alone. Ray had had a seizure once and in the emergency room they told me all about it. An epileptic can twitch all day long and you can leave him alone. It's not dangerous or at least not in the same way a heart attack is. In any case, there's not much to do if the epileptic is breathing. But this guy wasn't breathing. You could tell he wasn't breathing because he wasn't making any noise. It was strange to see him twitching and writhing there in complete silence. In the drill, you kneel down next to the doll and put your arm under its neck and push the head back. You do that to open the airway. I did that and it worked lickety-split. This man's tongue receded and he started coughing and gagging like there was no tomorrow. I was saved. I was saved because you can't do CPR on a person who is breathing no matter how much they're gagging or spitting blood or yellow stuff or whatever. I got up and went back into the store and stood behind the counter. A few minutes later, I started to go out again and see if the guy was really OK but by that time an ambulance had arrived and the cops were waving everyone away. I assume the guy made it to the hospital but then again maybe he didn't. In any case, I never heard a word about it.

Ray's seizure was a bit different, I recalled looking up at the sky. It was a bit different because he was Ray, but also because it happened in the middle of the night. There was no one else around except Lillian and she freaked out completely. Who can blame her? One minute she's sleeping peacefully next to Ray and the next she's wide awake with this body jerking and twitching and foaming beside her. Elizabeth was out of town. I don't know where Jack was. As I remember it, he slept through the whole thing. He never left his bed. He got up the next morning with no idea of what had taken place. But that doesn't make sense. Lillian was freaked out even though it had happened before. Or maybe she was freaked out *because* it had happened before. When it happened before, the doctors couldn't figure out what the problem was but put Ray on some medicine anyway. They never said he was an epileptic because if you say someone is an epileptic you have to take away that person's driver's license. In fact, they didn't have a clue as to whether Ray was an epileptic or not. They were trying to be kind. They put him on medicine and sent him home. In this case, he hadn't taken his medicine. He had gone out of town to see Elizabeth and forgot it. He took some as soon as he got back, but by that time, it was, evidently, too late. So Ray had this crazy seizure and Lillian freaked out. She grabbed me out of bed and brought me in to see. There Ray was jerking and twitching and drooling on the bed. He was making quite a bit of noise, so CPR was out of the question (thank god). I called an ambulance, but by the time it got there Ray had pretty much come out of it. He was, as you can imagine, a bit stunned but very calm. I had to hand it to Ray. He knew how to keep his head. The ambulance guys took him to the hospital anyway. Lillian and I drove there in her little white car. The emergency room was more or less a circus—as I have since learned, it generally is—full of drunks and the victims of violence and asthmatic children. It was there that a doctor came out and explained to me how you could let an epileptic twitch all day without there being too much danger. A seizure is something you have to let pass. There's no point in calling an ambulance as long as the epileptic is breathing. Then Ray came out and we all went home. As I remember it, Jack was still asleep in bed when we got there. But that doesn't make sense. He must have been someplace else.

The phone rang. It was morning. I got out of the hotel bed feeling like shit. I showered and changed. My bleeding knee had left marks all over the sheet. I got breakfast in a diner off the lobby, paid the bill and jumped into the rental. I pulled out of the lot and a couple of minutes later was moving at freeway speeds with the desert on either side and the mountains way off on the horizon in front. There wasn't a cloud in the sky and the sun was pounding down on everything like there was no tomorrow.

Ray and Lillian were in a little house at the foot of those mountains, a stone's throw from the highway, I thought, flying down the freeway with the desert on either side and the mountains way off on the horizon in front. From here, it was a straight shot. There's still quite a bit of freeway between this hotel and Ray and Lillian' house at the foot of the mountains. The freeway runs absolutely straight to the mountains. There's nothing between this hotel and Ray and Lillian' little house at the foot of the mountain except the curve of the Earth and that bit of freeway. If it weren't for the curve of the earth, I thought, I would be able to see Ray and Lillian' little house from here. It would be a little dark spot at the foot of the mountains. What's more, if it weren't for the curve of the earth, Ray and Lillian would be able to see this hotel. It would be a tiny dark bump beside the impossibly thin line of the freeway. If it weren't for the curve of the earth, I thought, there would be nothing between Ray and Lillian and I but space with the freeway running right through it, an extremely elongated wedge, tapering to a single point at the horizon. It would look like an arrow, I thought.

Once Lillian had an accident on the freeway, I recalled, flying down the freeway with the desert on either side and the mountains way off in front. It was a big deal. An accident at freeway speeds creates the possibility of fatality. It's a matter of inertia. If your car stops suddenly, at freeway speeds, your body just keeps going. In the case of Lillian, the accident was not fatal. It was snowing. Jack and Elizabeth were in the car. I wasn't there. We were children. Lillian was taking them to Ray in the hospital. There was a snowstorm. The snow was falling in big flakes and swirling around on every side. I wasn't there. I don't know where I was. Ray had had a seizure some time before. It was the first one and the most violent. The violence of the seizure had broken his arm. He woke up in bed beside Lillian, had a seizure and broke his arm. She took him to the hospital and the doctors said he must have a tumor in there, somewhere on his brain. They said straighten out your affairs and come back and we'll check it out and operate if we have to. This was in the days before CAT scans. In those days, if you wanted to look at someone's brain, you had to open the skull right up and take a look. When you opened up someone's skull, in those days, you didn't know what was going to happen next. If you find a tumor, you have to cut it out then and there. That's why Ray had to straighten out his affairs. So Ray did. He went home and straightened out his affairs. Then he went back for the operation. That's why he was in the hospital. That's why Lillian and Jack and Elizabeth were racing along at freeway speeds through a snowstorm to see him. I don't know where I was. We lived in a big house on a dirt road. Nobody was around. Nobody we knew. But I was in that house when Lillian was out on the freeway in the snowstorm with Jack and Elizabeth, racing along at freeway speeds to see Ray in the hospital. Where else could I have been? The accident happened to them: Lillian, Jack and Elizabeth. It didn't happen to me. I heard about it. It doesn't make sense. I was maybe six at the time. Nonetheless when they were having the accident, I was at home in the big house on the dirt road. No one else was around—no one we knew. Ray was in the hospital. I was alone. So they opened up Ray's skull to look at his brain. Actually they didn't open up the whole thing— too risky. Instead they drilled a hole on the top. A small hole on the top isn't as risky as opening up the whole thing. Those doctors knew what they were doing. They knew what they were doing but they didn't know what would happen. As far as what would happen went, those doctors didn't have a clue. That's why Ray had to straighten up his affairs. They drilled a hole in the top of Ray's skull and then they blew a bubble. They blew a bubble through the hole right around Ray's brain. I was at home when they were doing this. Lillian was driving at freeway speeds through a snowstorm with Jack and Elizabeth in back. She was praying. That's the part of the story everyone remembers. Lillian was saying Hail Mary's and what's more she was telling Jack and

Elizabeth to say Hail Mary's too. It was the time they all said Hail Mary's. That's how they remember it. They were saying Hail Mary's and then they had an accident. The doctors blew the bubble to look for bumps. The idea was that they could detect any bumps on the bubble—bumps from a tumor. Big bumps or small bumps. Even really small bumps would show up. Lord knows how they did it. Maybe they ran a current through the bubble. Why not? If you drill a hole in someone's skull and blow a bubble right around his brain, you may as well run a current through it. All bets are off at that point. That's why Ray had to straighten out his affairs. The car spun around a few times and came to rest in a ditch. It was totaled. But Lillian, Elizabeth and Jack crawled out without a scratch on them. I was at home. No tumor. No explanation. Ray had a seizure. The violence of the seizure broke his arm. They drilled a hole in his head and blew a bubble around his brain to find the tumor, but they didn't find anything. Maybe scar tissue, they thought. Maybe he'd been kicked by a horse, they thought. Back on the farm, he might have been kicked by a horse and now the scar tissue gave him a seizure that broke his arm. He was recovering. When Lillian, Jack and Elizabeth finally got there, he was recovering. The car was in a ditch somewhere with snow falling on it. I was in the big house on the dirt road all by myself. No one around—no one we knew. It got really late. They called me on the phone. The snow was falling around the big house too. I could see big flakes of snow whirling around in the darkness outside the kitchen window. They called me on the phone. Lillian's voice came out of the receiver. We had an accident, Lillian said. We all said Hail Mary's, Lillian said. Everyone's all right, Lillian said. And they were, I thought, flying down the freeway with the desert on either side and the mountains way off in front.

I can't let Lillian see my knee, I thought, driving at freeway speeds straight through the desert toward the foot of the mountains. If she sees it, she won't leave me alone about it, I thought. In matters of sickness, Lillian still treated me like a child. My body was hers to inspect as if I were a child. She'll want to look at my knee. She'll want to put a bandage on it. She'll make me talk to her about it. She won't understand that there is nothing to be done. You can't put a bandage on that kind of sore. It just makes things worse. All you can do is wait until it scabs over. I don't like talking about it, but Lillian would make me talk about it. She would make me explain why you couldn't put a bandage on it. The best thing to do would be to wear shorts. My jeans kept chaffing the sore and opening it up. I had put a fresh pair on before leaving the hotel but already the knee was all stiff and hard with dried blood. I didn't wear shorts because I didn't want other people to see the sore. My knee would disgust anyone who saw it. It made me uncomfortable to be the object of someone else's disgust even in this small way. It made me more uncomfortable than the sore itself, which really didn't hurt, just itched like crazy. I knew I would have to wear shorts eventually, but I wanted to do it in private. If I walked around in public with shorts on and my knee all bloody, people would be disgusted. But not only that, some of those people would be moved to ask about it. Maybe they thought there was some big adventure behind my bleeding knee. The truth would be a real let down. Besides it irritated me to discuss my sickness even with Lillian, to say nothing of discussing it with a perfect stranger I met at some gas station, for example. Of course, that person wouldn't consider himself a perfect stranger—not after seeing my knee. Once some perfect stranger saw my bleeding knee, he would feel he had a right to ask about it, even an obligation to ask about it. It's amazing, I thought, once someone knows you are sick or injured in any way, you can throw your privacy right out the window. Of course I couldn't walk around with an open wound forever—especially with my jeans chaffing it all day long. If you walk around with an open wound long enough, it'll get infected. Most infections aren't too bad but septicemia, for example, is no joke. An infected knee is no big deal, but infected blood can kill you. If you have infected blood, you have to get to a hospital right away and if there's no hospital to go to, you're fucked, as they say. I didn't know how long it would take to get septicemia, but I figured it was probably a long time. It wasn't a matter of gestation, I thought. It didn't grow into you until it got bad enough to kill you like most infections. It was more a matter of the likelihood of getting it increasing as time went on. Once you got it, it went everywhere instantly. It was in your blood for god's sake. But it could take months before that was likely to happen. The chances are small now, infinitesimally small, I thought, driving at freeway speeds straight through the desert toward the foot of the mountains.

If Ray has forgotten, he has forgotten completely, I thought, flying down the freeway with desert on both sides and the mountains in front way off on the horizon. He will have forgotten not only whatever it was that he had to tell me but also that he'd even called me up to get me to come down there to hear it. Ray was still sharp the last time I saw him. He was as sharp as anyone though he didn't always let on. He sounded sharp on the phone. I would like to think Ray will stay sharp right to the end. It would be a cheat not to. He's stayed sharp his whole life through everything; it would be a cheat to give out in the end. To give out at the end, even the very end, the very moment, would cheat him out of a whole life of staying sharp. Even if he wanted it, it would be a cheat. He might want it even if it were a cheat. It might not matter. Things can always get pretty bad. What's more they can get pretty bad really quickly.

71

They can get pretty bad *without warning*, as they say. Doctors think they know everything, and they do; but they only know everything *after the fact*. After the fact, it's easy for doctors to say: this is no surprise; we saw it coming. After the fact, everything becomes as clear as day and no one can believe they hadn't seen it before. In fact, they had seen it before. They saw everything including how bad it was going to get. They saw it all—to every last detail. But what they saw, they saw in the future. They saw it coming but they didn't see it here. Things that are coming are always fundamentally different than the very same things when they are here. If you say you saw it coming, you saw it coming but it wasn't the same thing that arrived. For example, Ray's grade school teacher went blind. He took us to see her when we visited the farm. She had diabetes. At that time, when you got diabetes, you knew you'd go blind. With this kind of diabetes, going blind was inevitable if you lived long enough. She knew she'd go blind if she lived long enough. But how could she anticipate blindness? It's not like keeping your eyes closed. It was extremely hot and bright the day he took us to see her. Jack came too. The sunlight was thick all over the yard. We saw her in a dark parlor in the front of her house. She was blind. We went back to the farm to meet his blind teacher and there she was in the dark parlor in the front of her house, blind. You could see her blindness in her hands. Illuminated on the coffee table by a crack in the curtains, her hands—by the way they interrupted the light—said she was blind. Their acquaintance was so far back that Ray had been a child, but she remembered him. She could see back then. They remembered each other. They talked for quite a while. Jack and I went out in the killing sunshine. It drained us completely. We were wandering around in the back yard looking at the bees. The sunshine pushed every particle of energy out of our bodies. Then Ray came out. We said goodbye to his blind teacher. Our limbs were like sludge. We must've passed out in the car. Some time later, she died. Ray mentioned it to us. Someone called him on the phone, and then he told us straight off the bat, my blind teacher is dead.

I started thinking about the other desert—the one in the hot, poor country where I lived with the moulay and Ali and Mou. That desert wasn't much different from this one. Certainly they were comparable at least in terms of size, I thought. It had been crazy of me to think I could've walked to the mountains on the horizon in that desert in a single day. Here I was driving toward the mountains in this desert at freeway speeds and the trip was going to take hours. I don't know what had gotten into me that morning. It never occurred to me when I set out that the distance I was planning to cover might simply be too long. I walked for hours making no discernable progress before I even had doubts. I only began to get an inkling when, after I'd gone what I figured should've been half way, I decided to look back. It wasn't that long after I had left the man, but already his house had vanished completely. It had sunk right into the ground. In fact, I could barely make out the town I'd left. It was just a little bump way out on the horizon and it wasn't right behind me. I started to worry about getting lost.

It's true I had meant to walk in pretty much a straight line from the town to the mountains, but looking back, I could see that I'd been zigzagging. I had wanted to walk straight across the plain that looked empty. But instead I'd been zigzagging from bush to bush or rock to rock. From the town, there appeared to be no obstructions, and at the same time, there appeared to be no landmarks. As it turned out, there were landmarks, loads them. There was a rock, a bush, or even a patch of tough grass with a tree growing out of it every hundred yards or so. What's more, as it turned out, on the plain, I had been drawn toward every one of those landmarks. I wanted to walk in a straight line to the mountains but the mountains were no good as a landmark; they took up the entire horizon; away from the town, every way led to the mountains. From the town the plain appeared to be completely empty. But you can't walk toward nothing. If you are walking *toward*, you have to be walking toward *something*. I could walk toward a rock or a bush or a solitary tree, but I couldn't walk toward the mountains—every way went toward the mountains—and I couldn't walk toward the emptiness between the mountains and the town. Instead, I had zigzagged from bush to rock to tree or from tree to rock to bush or from rock to bush to tree or from tree to bush to rock. I had zigzagged right into this emptiness, I thought looking back for the town way out on the horizon.

There is no one around for miles, I had thought, standing in the middle of that desert so long ago. I could see for miles, and there was no one there. I didn't really want to run into anyone, but still the emptiness was oppressive. What's more, the silence was oppressive. I started singing to myself. No one can hear me, I thought. There was no one around. I could see for miles and there was no one there. But even if I did see someone—a small dark shape on the plain, say a half a mile away—that person still wouldn't be able to hear me. He'd see me if he was looking but he wouldn't hear anything. I could sing at the top of my lungs and no one would hear me. You can't hear a person singing from a half a mile away even if you can see them. The sound of your voice travels out in a circle. A quiet sound makes a small circle. A loud sound makes a big circle. But no sound goes on forever. You don't need a wall or a hill or a forest to block the sound; it dies all by itself. There could be a hundred people, I thought— walking again towards the mountains, singing to myself— standing around at different points on this plain, singing at the top of their lungs. I might be able to see them—I could see for miles—but I wouldn't hear them. And they wouldn't hear me. Not one of them would hear me because the energy would go out of the sound of my voice before it could reach them.

Thank god it's not the summer, I thought, walking again towards the mountains, singing to myself. The summer went off in that place like an atom bomb. I had only seen the town in the summer once. I had left the town in the spring but then came back in the summer to get some things. I had been gone only a matter of weeks. It wasn't so bad when I left, but when I came back, the summer had squashed everything flat. I showed up in the afternoon. It was extremely hot. Everything was covered in dust. Nothing moved. There was absolutely no one around. The air had thinned to almost nothing with heat and silence. This is what atom bombs do, I thought. I made my way to the concrete box where I and the moulay had lived without seeing a soul. The sound of my footsteps shot through the thinness of the air and ricocheted around the village before careening out and further out into the silence of the plain. When I wrenched open the metal door to our box, the noise was deafening. Two weeks of neglect had destroyed the apartment. Everything was covered in sand and what was not covered in sand was covered in dust. The moulay and I had gassed the place before I left and shoveled up pile after pile of dead cockroaches with an old newspaper. Nonetheless hundreds scattered when I turned on the light. The fecundity of the cockroaches in this dry place where there was nothing but dust and sand appalled me. All of this eating with nothing to eat, I thought. I didn't sit down there. I killed the rest of the afternoon at a table under an awning beside the taxi stand drinking Nescafe and staring at the street. I returned to the apartment after dark. Before I slept, I turned my sleeping bag inside out to make sure nothing had got inside it. Still, I was up for hours. I awoke the next morning to the soft pelting of flies against my face, I recalled, walking again towards the mountains, singing to myself.

As I walked, I recalled, the setting sun sucked the color right out of the landscape all around me. Everything became very gray. It looked like the moon. I stopped. Over my shoulder, I could see my own shadow stretching a hundred yards behind me. The mountains still hadn't gotten any closer. They might be a hundred miles away, I thought. It was idiotic to think I could ever reach them on foot. I knew I had to go back. I had stopped singing some time ago. You can't sing forever. I stopped after I had noticed that I couldn't hear myself. I had been singing and singing and listening and listening but then at some point I stopped listening and then a while later, I stopped singing. When I had been singing and listening, I had also been thinking. I was thinking if you listen to someone's voice, you should be able to see the person in your head. If you could hear the voice then, in your head, you should be able to see the person. It's funny I had always considered this a fact but at the same time I knew it wasn't true. I knew it wasn't true because I always listened to people on the bus. I listened to their voices, and in my head, I saw them. Once I listened to this man talking and talking for hours in a seat behind me on the bus. The bus was a mess. It was a cross-country trip. A pack of old cigarettes was wedged between the seat cushions beside me. I drifted in and out of sleep but I could always here him talking, and in my head, I could see his face. I could see his arms and his hands. The bus rode on and on, and the man talked on and on, and I could hear his voice and in my head, I could see him—his face, his arms, his hands—the whole person—talking on the seat behind me. But when it came time to get off and I stood up and looked, the person behind me was someone else entirely. Someone else entirely had been doing all that talking. Walking across the plain, I had been singing and singing and listening and listening but after a while I stopped listening because in my head, I couldn't see anyone. A while after that, I stopped singing. I listened to my voice for quite some time but in my head I saw no one. I didn't see someone entirely different from myself. I saw no one at all, I had thought, walking, silently, toward the orange mountains way off on the horizon. That was when I first realized I hadn't the faintest clue as to who I was.

The whole world of the freeway with the desert rushing by on both sides and the mountains looming in front popped out of existence like a bubble of soap the very moment I got out of the car. I was at a gas station. Sunlight was crashing all over the place. It was really hot and mostly still except for the sounds of engines and the rush of cars passing on the freeway. Straight away I noticed a man in dark glasses smoking in front of the shop. I noticed him straight away because he was looking at me. He was staring at my knee. I could tell by the incline of his head. I didn't look at the man. I grabbed a nozzle from the pump and walked over to the rental, but as I filled the rental, I could feel him looking at me. He couldn't see my knee—or the dark patch of blood-soaked denim above my knee—because it was against the side of the rental. The rental was hot. I burned my hand on the chrome above the wheel. It took a long time to fill up. I wasn't watching the numbers click upwards on the pump because the man was on the other side smoking in front of the shop, and I didn't want to look at him. I was looking over the top of the rental at the road and the desert beyond it. I had to squint. The sunlight was blinding. When the nozzle finally clicked and gulped, I turned around to replace it by the pump. The man was gone. I was relieved. He had finished his cigarette and took off, I thought. I went into the shop to pay. Walking into the air conditioning was like stepping into a pool of cool water. All the noise from outside stopped the moment the door fell closed behind me. The man was there. There he was, first in line at the cash register. I got in line and waited. The man paid and turned to leave, but then paused in front of the glass door. He took off his glasses to wipe them on his shirt. His eyes were extraordinarily blue. His eyes were as blue as the water in the pool at the hotel. He saw me staring at him. He said, I know you. You're the guy from the plane, he said. You stole my fucking Dictaphone.

Something started whirring against my chest.

I can hear it whirring in your breast pocket, the man said. Don't deny it. It's there. I can hear it. It's recording everything I say. Say, that's funny. Usually I use that Dictaphone to record everyone else, but here you are, using it to record me. It's ironic. But I'm glad I ran into you. What are the chances of that? It's a lucky break for me. Now I can get my Dictaphone back. Don't worry I'm not mad. As it turns out, I haven't needed it. Apart from running into you here, this trip has been bad luck from beginning to end. First there was the loss of my Dictaphone, then I got sick as a dog, then I couldn't find a hamburger to save my life, and worst of all, when I tried to call up my client, I found out he was dead. Just like that. He was fine the last time I saw him. Heart attack. It happened in his living room. He drew his last breath writhing in agony under a coffee table. It happened six hours before I tried to call him. I got his secretary. She told me flat out: he's dead. Your client is dead. This whole trip has been a waste of time. But now I've run into you. Maybe things are looking up. Just when I thought the whole trip was a wash, I run into you and can get my Dictaphone back. What are the chances? Hey, you know what this is? This is a good omen. You might think that's a lot of crap, but I believe it. All you have to do is pay attention. Once you start paying attention, you'll find omens everywhere. Good omens and bad omens. I once stayed in bed for a week because I'd noticed a bad omen. It saved my life. So they're going to bury my client under a rock in the mountains out there. He wanted it that way. That's why I'm driving out here in the middle of nowhere. I'm going to pay my respects. Don't get the idea I'm all broken up about it. I didn't actually know my client that well. It was all business between us. Still I want to pay my respects. It's the least I can do. I never miss a funeral if I can avoid it—even when the dead person was someone I hardly knew, even if the dead person was just a name on a piece of paper to me. I always go to the funeral if I can. It's bad luck to miss one. And there's the business aspect as well. You meet people at funerals. If it's the funeral of a client, there's a good chance the people there won't be much different from your client. If they're not that much different, they might make good clients too. I never bring it up, but people remember. You remember people you meet at funerals. I've had people call me out of the blue years later. They remembered me. They remembered me from the funeral. So I guess I'll need that little baby back now. You can just take it out of your pocket. Or I can get it. Here, that's it, isn't it? Oh yes, that's definitely it. Thanks for keeping it clean, buddy. Hey it's still running. Don't worry about the batteries I have a whole box in the car. I'll just—

The tape ran out and the machine clicked off. I put it back in the medicine cabinet behind the mirror. Do you need some help? Lillian said from the living room. I squirted some medicine out of a tube and rubbed it all over my knee. I was wearing shorts. My knee was still a bloody mess. No, I said.

I can't stay in here forever, I was thinking, sitting on the closed toilet, looking down into the tub. You can go to the bathroom to get away. You can sit here for a while, but you can't stay here forever. What's more I can't stay in this house. Everything has been a mistake. I never should have come here, and now I can't stay. It would have been better to decline. Ray waited his whole life to ask me to come. I came. I flew half way around the world to hear what he had to say, but now, in this bathroom, with Lillian right outside the door and Ray on the porch, I knew I should have declined. I would decline now if I could but now it was too late. You can't decline an invitation after you have arrived. Declining it when he made it—over the phone, half way around the world—would have been bad, but declining it now is completely out of the question. Why are you here then? they might ask. Why did you come? You don't fly half way around the world to say you're not coming. It doesn't make sense. What's wrong with you? You can't leave now. You have to stay. You said you were going to come, and now here you are. You have to stay. You can't just walk out of it, I thought.

When I was in kindergarten, I recalled, sitting on the closed toilet, looking down into the tub, I had this leopard suit. I got it for Halloween. You wore it like pajamas. It covered my whole body, even my head. It was a great suit. It wasn't the kind of costume you put over your clothes. It was the kind of costume that *was* your clothes. I jumped and pounced all morning. Then we went to kindergarten. After the party, they told me to take it off. But I couldn't take it off because there was nothing under it. There was nothing under it except my body. They wanted me to take it off but I couldn't so I went to the bathroom. I didn't take it off there. I crawled through the open window. They found me wandering by the road, I'm told. Everyone thought I was trying to walk home. Nobody knew about the suit. To them, it was just crazy. They thought I was trying to walk home, but I'm not so sure, now, that that was where I was going. I think I was headed for the jungle.

The kindergarten teacher was absolutely nuts, I recalled looking down into the tub. She had this sponge. She said, on the cross, Christ asked for water but they gave him vinegar instead. They put the vinegar in the sponge. He asked for water but they gave him vinegar instead. Taste it, she said. She was off her head. I can still remember her face. It was the face of a crazy person. I can see it even now as clear as day. I can always tell when a person is off their head. I don't even have to look at their faces. I can feel it if they're close. If someone's off their head and standing not too far away from me, I can feel it right off the bat. That person doesn't even have to open his mouth. I can feel their craziness in the air. I can feel it right through my clothes. It's repulsive. Crazy people are repulsive. There was this girl I met at a wedding. She was off her head and I knew it. We sat at the same table. She was talking to someone else but she kept looking at me out of the corner of her eye. She was off her head. I could feel it as plain as day. I knew she was off her head, and what's more she knew I knew. This person is completely crazy, I thought. I didn't need to hear a word she said. She knew I knew. It was like a secret between us. She kept looking over at me, and her look said, you know I'm crazy and what's more I know you know. It was our little secret at that wedding. They say if you think you are crazy, you are probably not crazy. That's a crock. Crazy people *know* they are crazy. What's more crazy people don't want anyone else to know they are crazy. Crazy people will *move mountains* as they say or *go to the ends of the Earth* as they say to keep sane people from knowing they are crazy. Who wouldn't? But it's all a waste of time. Or it's mostly a waste of time. You can fool a lot of people but you can't fool everyone. At this wedding, for example, I and the crazy girl both knew she was crazy. But no one else had a clue. They were completely oblivious. No one there had a clue that she was crazy except her and me. I could feel it. I was repulsed, and she hated me for it. I could feel her hate as well as her craziness. I could feel it right through my clothes. It felt like heat. Weeks later, I heard about this girl. They had found her wandering around a bus station late at night utterly naked. She was completely nuts. They sent her home. They sent her home lickety-split, I thought looking down into the bathtub with Lillian out in the hall and Ray on the porch in back.

Everyone is safe back home, I thought looking down into the tub. They're sleeping now, I thought. The world has turned, and everyone back home is now on the sleeping half. I'm on the half that's wide-awake. Nancy is sleeping. The girls are sleeping. The tortoises are scratching around in their tray. The apartment is dark and silent except for sleeping noises and the noise of the tortoises scratching around in their tray. A loud noise would be unthinkable in that sleeping apartment. It would destroy the place. It wouldn't be just a matter of waking everyone up. A loud noise would cut through the walls and ceilings and floors. The apartment would crack right open and Nancy and the girls would tumble into the crack along with the falling rubble. I should be there with them, I thought looking down into the tub. I should be there with them in that sleeping apartment either asleep or awake in the living room looking down on the city of sleeping people. The silence of the apartment is strong, almost impenetrable—a loud noise is unthinkable—but still they would be safer if I were with them. I would be safer if I were with them in the silence of that sleeping apartment on the other side of the world. Impossible things are happening all around us all the time, I thought looking down into the tub. The impossible pushes into

82

the possible at every point. All an impossible thing has to do to become possible—indeed to become commonplace—is happen; and it is happening all around us all the time. Every commonplace thing was impossible before it happened. This bathtub was impossible, I thought, looking down into the tub. But here it is. I haven't seen Ray and Lillian in years. For years, it was impossible to see Ray and Lillian. For years, I never even thought of seeing Ray and Lillian. What was the point? It was impossible. It was impossible to fly half way around the world to see them. But here I am, I thought looking down into the tub. And now it has become commonplace. Lillian was waiting outside the door with her snacks in their plastic boxes. Ray was waiting on the porch with the information he was waiting to impart to me, if he hadn't forgotten it. It would be impossible for him to forget but if he did forget, that would become commonplace. Ray would go from always being sharp to having given out. It would be a cheat but that would hardly matter. Ray would have been cheated out of a whole life of staying sharp. I have already been cheated out of years and years of not visiting them. We would both be cheated but that would hardly matter. I have visited him, and if he has forgotten his call, he has given out. It's as if we never lived, I thought looking down into the tub. We thought we had lived. Ray thought he had stayed sharp and I thought I had stayed away, but instead, I had visited and he had given out. The person who stayed sharp and the person who stayed away never lived. Instead the person who gave out and the person who visited lived, were living at this very moment.

I had this dream when I was a kid, I recalled, sitting on the closed toilet, looking down into the tub. I had wandered off. I was out walking in the high grass behind our house when I stumbled into a sitting room laid out there in the middle of the field. It was just a rug, a couple of chairs and an old coffee table flattening a square of grass in the middle of the field. I stumbled into it. The grass had grown around this flattened patch like walls. It was a gray day. I had wandered off. I had wandered off away from the house through the high grass in the field when I stumbled into the sitting room laid out there in the middle someplace. Everything was filthy, of course, but everything was also intact. There was a coffee table, a couple of chairs and a rug just sitting out there in the middle of the field surrounded by grass. The grass grew around it like walls. It was then that I first remembered the dream. I was a boy in the dream, and there were two giants—Ray and Lillian. The giants were made of acrobats. The acrobats stood on each other's shoulders. That's how they made them up—Ray and Lillian. One giant was Lillian, and the other was Ray. Each of the giants wanted me to join it. Each of the giants wanted to incorporate me into the team of acrobats that made it up. I panicked completely. I went blind with fear. I ran. They reached for me—both of them, at the same time. I jumped into a toy box and pulled down the lid. The lid had pictures of pirates on it. I fell through the bottom and woke up instantly. I woke up the instant the lid shut. I had jumped straight through the bottom of that box right into the waking world.

I left the bathroom. There was no point in staying there any longer. I went out into the living room. I was heading toward the porch but Lillian was standing in front of the sliding glass doors, talking a mile a minute. I stood right in front of her but I couldn't hear a word she said.

She thinks I hear everything, I thought, standing in front of Lillian but not hearing a word she said. But actually I've heard nothing or at least very little. My whole life Lillian has stood right in front of me just like this talking a mile a minute and the whole time she thought I was hearing everything when in fact I've heard nothing at all—or very little. At this point, I thought, Lillian must think I know everything. She thinks I know everything she has been telling me all these years I have stood right in front of her not hearing a word she says. It's amazing that there's anything left. She's been talking to me like this for years—my whole life—at a mile a minute with me standing right in front of her hearing, she thought, every word she said. How could there be anything left? You'd think she'd have said it all, at this point. You'd think at this point Lillian could just be silent when I stand in front of her. You'd think she could be silent and reflecting. She could be silent and reflecting on everything she had already told me, and I too could be silent and reflecting on everything she thinks I've heard. Or maybe she knows. Maybe she knows I never hear a word she says, but it simply doesn't matter. Some things don't matter. Or maybe they do but there's nothing you can do about them so you go on doing whatever it is you do regardless of the thing that matters. If you could do something about the thing that mattered you would, but you can't so you do something else. It doesn't really matter whatever you do, but you do it anyway. Lillian's father was a drunk, for example. But he had his good points. He was a drunk the whole time Lillian was a girl, but he wasn't only a drunk. He built the Panama Canal, for example. He dug it with a shovel. He did that before he got married. He built other things. He was a person who built things. Even as a drunk he managed to build things. Lillian's mother was scared of him. She locked him out of the house. She took the kids and hid them in a closet. There were three of them at that time. Three girls, can you imagine? All those women crammed into a small closet in that tiny apartment with Lillian's father, the drunk, rampaging outside or pleading. Or singing? Who knows? He might have been singing. Lillian's mother was afraid of him, but Lillian found him cheerful. He was cheerful, happy-go-lucky, as they say, and a drunk and he built things. He built her a bedroom in the attic, for example. He dug the Panama Canal. Their apartment was a small place. There were four women living there along with Lillian's father, the drunk. She had two sisters, and of course, her mother was there as well, but Lillian's father built the bedroom in the attic for Lillian. It was her room in that crowded place. He died of a heart attack in someone's living room. I don't know if Lillian ever visited his grave. Her mother kept away from it. Lillian hasn't said. Or if she has mentioned it, I didn't hear her. I don't think it could be any other way, I thought standing in front of Lillian not hearing a word she said. I started thinking about Nancy.

Nancy is sleeping and the apartment is silent but there's nothing peaceful about it, I thought, standing right in front of Lillian without hearing a word she said. It's not peaceful because Nancy is having nightmares. The nightmares are pushing out around the surface of her body. The peace of the silent apartment would be complete if it weren't for the nightmares pushing out around the surface of Nancy's body. She twitches occasionally and mumbles. It's clear she's dreaming. What's more, it's clear her dreams are nightmares. Nancy has nightmares every night. Sometimes she remembers the nightmares; sometimes she doesn't. But I always see them pushing out around the surface of her body when she is asleep. They're pushing out from someplace else. They don't come from the waking world—or at least, they don't come directly. It's true every day of Nancy's waking life is a nightmare. People are constantly trying to push her face in it or take advantage. What's more, every day is a different nightmare. But Nancy never succumbs to any of these daytime nightmares because she's too quick. Nancy moves quickly all day long dodging whatever nightmare it is that the day has to offer. She's quick and she's successful. But at night, she has no choice but to slow down. Every night she slows down until she is nearly still. In the process of becoming still, every joint in her body cracks in a long arrhythmic series of clicks and twitches. You can see the last of the remaining motion leaking out of her body in twitches, and then she mumbles. It's clear she's dreaming and what's more it's clear her dreams are nightmares—a different nightmare for every night. I have nightmares too. But my nightmares are always the same nightmare. My days are as different as anyone else's but my nightmares are always the same. For me, there's only one nightmare. There is only one nightmare, and it never changes. My nightmare has grown so monotonous in its singularity that I can hardly see it anymore. At one time, it was concentrated and distinct. But now it is diffuse and unidentifiable. It has receded. It has faded into the background, as they say. And as it has receded, it has become ubiquitous. It's in the very air, as they say. First the air became saturated with the nightmare, and then as time went on, the nightmare supersaturated the air. I can't see it anymore, but it's there, in the air, and what's more, there is more of it in the air than the air can truly hold. This is an inherently unstable situation. The situation is a fluid waiting for a catalyst to make it solid. The catalyst might be anything. It might be a bit of string or a grain of sand. When it comes, everything will change, I thought standing right in front of Lillian but not hearing a word she said.

The doorbell rang. Lillian shut up and moved from in front of me to get the door. The path to the porch was clear. I stepped out through the glass doors to join Ray. He was sitting on a rock looking out over the cactus in the wash below. The mountains were behind us somewhere, looming over the house. I'm glad you're here, Ray said looking out over the cactus in the wash. I didn't think you'd make it and if you did I thought it might be too late. I tried writing it down but every time I did, I had to edit what I had written to the point where it didn't make any sense. But don't worry. It's all up here, Ray said pointing to his forehead.

I waited a long time I know, Ray said, sitting on a rock looking out over the cactus in the wash below. But just because I waited doesn't mean I forgot. I haven't forgotten anything. I haven't forgotten a single word. I know with all this time passing, you think you've moved on, but you haven't. Time is like distance; it disappears after you get there. You can drive a thousand miles and the whole world feels like the inside of a car. It feels like it will go on forever. It feels like there's nothing else. You can drive hour after hour like that and to you, in the car, driving, the time when you were outside of the car—so long ago and so far away—will feel like a dream. There's only the car at that point. There's nothing but the car. Even the road rushing by outside with clouds and telephone poles or what have you is part of the car. The car becomes your whole world. But, I'll tell you what. The very moment you get out, it's all over; and a moment after that it's like it never was. Time is like that, or I should say duration. No matter how long it goes on when it's over, it disappears. Things get so heavy. They get ungodly heavy. Things can get so heavy you think you'll never move again amidst all those heavy things. It's duration that does it. The longer something goes on, the heavier it gets. If it went on forever, it would get infinitely heavy. But it never does. And when it's over, piff!

When I was little, Ray said sitting on rock looking down on the cactus in the wash, I hit this guy with a hammer. He was big. I snuck up behind him with a claw hammer and let him have it right on the bean. I hit him because he was teasing. I was maybe six. He worked on our farm. All the farm hands were sitting in a circle playing cards and this one hand was teasing me because I was six. I guess it got to me. I didn't say anything but it got to me. It got to me to the point where I had to do something. So I snuck away and found this hammer. I had been hanging around them but then I snuck away. I came back with it behind my back. I came back to the circle. The hands were all there. They were still playing cards. The guy who was teasing me was there. He was playing cards. I let him have it right on the bean. It hurt I'll bet. He was none too pleased. The other hands thought it was hilarious. It didn't kill him. I was only six for god's sake. It didn't seriously injure him but it pissed him off. He didn't have to stick around for that. He took off. He turned his back and left the farm. He left that very night. We forgot all about him. Or rather, they forgot all about him, but I didn't forget all about him. The whole farm forgot all about the guy I hit with the hammer. They all forgot except me. I know they forgot because they were surprised when he came back. Just like that. Out of the blue. A couple of years later, this guy showed up. It was the same one who took off. It was the guy I hit with the hammer. He hadn't forgotten it. I could tell just by looking at his face. I took one look into his face and the moment I had hit him with the hammer came back as if all the time he had been gone had never happened. I think he showed up because he wanted to get even. He wanted to get even with someone but there was no one to get even with. They had all forgotten, and I was only eight. He couldn't get even. The best he could do was demand his pancakes. He had left a bag of pancake flour when he took off a couple of years before, and now he wanted it back, just like that. My mother went and found it just where he had left it. She was like that. My mother was a troubled woman but she kept things in order. It was the farm that did it. If you live on a farm, you have to keep things in order. At the same time, the farm troubled her. In fact, it drove her nuts. It drove her straight out of her mind. It was the farm and all that flat space, and the wind. In those days in that place, the wind drove women out of their minds on a regular basis. You could hardly visit a farm in the county without finding a crazy woman on it. And the towns were worse. They were filled with women, and all those women were out of their minds. It was the wind. In the old days, they lived in sod houses and a single season was enough to push a woman straight over the brink. You couldn't get away from the wind, and if you could get away from the wind, you couldn't get away from the sound of the wind. In all that space, there was no place to go. No matter where you went, there was the wind or the sound of the wind. It drove the women crazy. Who knows what it did to the men? My family never lived in a sod house. We had a frame. It took longer, but the wind got to my mother anyway. She lived a long time for a woman in her situation but when she died she was still nuts. That was quite a stretch. In one part of her life she was sane but in the other part she was crazy. The part she was crazy lasted a long time. In any case, it's always the last part that counts. In the old days, the women died young. They died young, because when they were young, they had babies. Having babies back then in those sod houses was no joke. If the woman made it through the first one, she'd get killed on the second. If she made it through the second, she'd get killed on the third. It was only a matter of time. The bleeding did it. You can't have a baby without shedding a little blood, but if you shed a lot of blood you die. It doesn't matter how strong you are. You only have so much blood. If it leaks out of you, that's it. Your heart can't work on nothing. Your heart can't work on air. You can bet those women were strong as horses. They broke their backs keeping the farm in order; but then the wind drove them crazy, and it was the babies that killed them. The men kept going. They broke their backs too but they didn't go crazy and they didn't have babies. A man in those days could work his way past two or three wives. The wives would go crazy and die having babies but the men just kept going. They were breaking their backs long after their wives were in the ground. It's a mystery about the wind. It drove the wives crazy but the husbands stayed sane. It's a mystery. The men weren't deaf after all. Or maybe they did go crazy but it just didn't make any difference. No one really noticed. You can break your back all day out in a field someplace and be completely out of your mind, but who's going to notice? In the house, it's different. Or maybe the men did go crazy and people did know, but even though they knew, they chose to keep their mouths shut about it. No one knows. These days it's just the opposite. The men die young and the women keep going. Heart attacks do it. They kill off the men like flies but spare the women. Whoever heard of a woman having a heart attack? This place—Ray gestured widely—is chock full of women on their second or third husbands. They're on their second or third husband because their first or second husbands died. Their first or second husbands died of heart attacks. That's why people come here. They come here to die. Both the men and the women come here to die. It's warm here. In general, the weather is great. Both the men and the women want a warm place to die. They show up in this warm place in couples but the men die first and the women just keep going. What's more, nowadays it's the men who go crazy and the women who stay sane. It's craziness that kills the men and sanity that preserves their wives. Insanity causes heart attacks. It takes a long time but in the end that's what happens. A man goes crazy but he never lets on. For years, he never lets on. Crazy people—especially crazy men—don't want sane people to know they're crazy. They'll move mountains as they say or go to the ends of the Earth as they say to keep sane people from knowing they are crazy. Crazy men are especially reticent about their craziness. When a man goes crazy, he doesn't let on. Who would? He keeps it to himself. He can keep it to himself for years. He can keep it to himself right to the very end, and if nothing else happens in the meantime, it will be a heart attack that kills him, and you can bet that heart attack was caused by the insanity that he kept to himself. Whenever I hear so and so has had a heart attack, I know the odds are ten to one that that person was insane. Insanity will not be hidden. Insanity will not allow itself to be hidden. At least, it will not allow itself to be hidden forever. Insanity is a public thing. It needs to show. Insanity that doesn't show is hardly insanity at all. If insanity can't find any other way out into the open, it causes a heart attack. You can't get more public than that—almost. This guy I knew at the office went insane. He went insane early on but for years it didn't show. He kept it to himself for years. He got old and his wife got old and his children grew up and all the while he was completely out of his head, but it didn't show. He kept it to himself. All that time he was working and getting old and his wife was getting old and the children were growing up, this guy was completely insane. And then he stopped working but he was still insane and still keeping it to himself. He kept it to himself right up to the very end. It wasn't a heart attack. He blew his brains out. He left a note. It was absolutely deliberate. No one had a clue. He had planned it. He planned it the very moment he went off his head early on. From that point forward, it was just a matter of time. There was this moment early on, when this guy from the office went off his head and came up with the plan to blow his brains out, and he kept it. He kept that moment for years and years while he worked and grew old and his wife grew old and his children grew up and he stopped working and he moved out here. When he moved here, he still had that moment. You'd think in all that time, it would have gotten lost. You would think it would fall away into the background of his sane life that kept getting bigger and bigger as time went on and on. But that

92

moment didn't get lost. How could it? He was off his head. Instead his sane life fell into the background of the insanity that he had kept to himself, close to his chest, and it was that very same sane life that disappeared like a bubble of soap the very moment this guy blew his brains out, Ray said, sitting on a rock looking out over the cactus in the wash below.

Thank god for your sanity, Ray said, and thank god for your health. After all, without your health or without your sanity, there's not much left, is there? And it won't matter how long you were sane or how long you were healthy before, once you lose your health or your sanity, that's it. You can't put your sane life in a bank. You can't keep it safe for a rainy day. You could be sane for years and years—your whole life—and then go crazy, and you can kiss your sane life goodbye. It doesn't matter how long it was when it's over. When it's over it's gone. You may as well have been crazy your whole life for all your sane life means when it's over. Just look at your cousin! She was sane her whole life and then one night she started wrapping her parents' kitchen in plastic. There she was wrapping the entire kitchen in plastic. There she was wrapping up each fork and spoon. It was at night. Her parents went out. She went nuts. They left at night. When they left, she was sane, but when they came back, there she was in the dark kitchen wrapping plastic around the spoons. It happened at night. Just like that. It must've killed them. And now it's like she was nuts all along. It's like she was hiding it. It can't be easy. It can't be easy to be nuts but hiding it. That's got to take a lot of work. That's got to cause a lot of stress. It's enough to cause a heart attack. But what's the point? What's the point of doing all that work to hide your insanity, when all you have to do is slip up once and it will be like you had never hidden it at all? Besides, everybody knows. They know if you are crazy, but they don't let on. I can spot a crazy person from a mile away. I knew your cousin was crazy when she was six years old. I could see it plain as day. Everyone could. Everyone knew. But they never let on. They didn't let on because they didn't want to get involved. Who would? Besides, it's not nice to tell a crazy person that you have recognized his insanity. It pushes them right over the brink. They may have been crazy before but once they know someone else knows they're crazy, they get twice as crazy. There's nothing to be done. Just drugs and talk. But you know under all those drugs or under all that talk, the insanity is still there. It's there and waiting. It's waiting for the drugs to run out or the talk to stop to come right out again. Look at your cousin! She can hardly get up and move around under all those drugs. But even if she could get up and move around, she'd be up and moving around insane. There she is under all those drugs like a hundred blankets. All she wants to do is to be up and moving around but she doesn't want to be up and moving around because she doesn't want to be insane. Who would? Your mother used to work for the poor. She was poor but then she got out of it and worked for the poor. It was a good job. It was the best job she could get. But she stopped. She stopped because it was futile. She couldn't stand it, she says. She could stand the futility with the adults but she couldn't stand it with the children. When your mother was young, she lived like dirt. Her father was a drunk. She lived like dirt with her mother, her two sisters and her father, the drunk. All of them were hungry. Back then, the nuns put food in her mouth. They put food in her mouth, and they pushed her face in it. They put food in her mouth because she was poor, and they pushed her face in it because she was poor. Being poor is a kind of sin. You have to suffer for it. You have to suffer for it your whole life. If you are poor, someone will push your face in it. If no one is around to push your face in it, you have to do it yourself. Jesus never said, blessed are the poor. No sirree. Jesus said, blessed are the poor *in spirit.* By that, He meant morons. Morons don't care so much. You can push a moron's face in it all day long and he won't care. Or if he does, he'll forget. But the poor don't forget. It's a sin. The nuns were poor too and you can bet they got their faces pushed in it. That's the way it goes. It's a sin and you have to suffer. So, they put food in her mouth and pushed her face in it, but when I met them, your mother was all grown up and things were better. At least as far as money went. Your mother wasn't poor; she worked for the poor. Or rather, she worked for the state. Who's going to work for the poor? What are they going to pay you? She worked for the state. It was a good job. But she stopped because it was futile. When I proposed to your mother, her father was still a drunk. But he had his good points. He gave me a washing machine for example. He gave it to me to sell. The idea was I'd sell the machine and make some money. Then I'd buy another washing machine and sell that. I had some money before that but I had pissed it all away. I pissed it away because I was single. Single people piss their money away—especially single men. You work all day and piss your money away at night and then get up in the morning and make some more. I walked all over town with that washing machine. I put it in the back of my car. I'd park the car and walk from door to door trying to unload that washing machine. About the time your mother, her mother and her father became convinced there was no way I was going to get rid of that washing machine, I sold it. But it broke when I was lifting it out of the trunk. The money your mother's father had spent on the washing machine was pissed away. I did it. Then your mother and I got married. We were never poor, but at the same time, we never made it. If you make it, you're set. If you haven't made it, you worry. We worried. We worried we'd get poor. We worried we'd get our faces pushed in it. It's a sin. Worrying is a sin too but it isn't as bad as poverty. If you worry, you suffer. If you worry, you can't taste your food. You

95

put food in your own mouth and no one pushed your face in it but you can't taste it because you are worrying. I couldn't taste my food for my entire working life. I could only taste snacks. I ate tuna out of a can for twenty years but I never tasted it. I ate it standing by the kitchen counter after everyone had gone to bed, but I didn't taste it. I could only taste snacks. Even now I don't know what tuna tastes like. I don't have the foggiest notion. I'm not allowed to eat much now but I can tell you what I eat I taste. Even that low fat artificial crap, I taste. It's not as bad as you think but I'd prefer eggs. I'm sure I would taste them. I can taste them even now just thinking about it. I'd prefer a mess of eggs. A mess of eggs is more than three. I'd prefer a mess of eggs cooked in butter. But I'm not allowed to eat what I want. If I snuck off to a diner and had a big plate of eggs—a mess of eggs—cooked in butter, they'd have to take me out of the diner feet first. Heart attacks are in my blood. I had two brothers. One was bright and the other was good. A soldier killed the good one and the bright one had a heart attack. It's in our blood. If the soldier hadn't killed the good one, chances are a heart attack would have got him. If a combine hadn't killed my father, a heart attack would have got him. Heart attacks are in our blood. Yours too. The very blood your heart is pumping has a heart attack in it. And god knows what else. Some times I think it doesn't matter, but other times I think it does. In any case I quit smoking, Ray said sitting on a rock looking over the cactus in the wash below.

When you were a kid, you were afraid of the dark, Ray said, sitting on the rock, looking over the cactus in the wash below. You weren't afraid of something in the dark, you were afraid of the dark itself. It drove your mother and I nuts. You used to play in the basement. The basement was dark during the day and dark at night, but not so dark during the day. Although it was not strictly necessary you turned the lights on down there whether it

96

were day or night. You played in the basement with the lights on during the day, and when night came, you left them on. You never turned them off because you didn't want to walk back up the steps. You were afraid of the dark. The lights on down in the basement drove us crazy. The idea of the lights burning down there all night long in the empty basement drove us nuts. The waste drove us nuts and the money but it was the waste more than the money. But you were a kid. Waste didn't mean much to you and money meant nothing at all. We told you to turn off the lights, but you ignored us. We wondered what the big deal was. After all you had to go down in the dark to turn the lights on in the first place, didn't you? It didn't make sense. But I thought about it for a long time and finally I figured it out. It was like this: The light switch was at the end of the hall. During the day, you could go downstairs and plunge into the darkness all the way to the end of the hall to turn on the lights, no problem. It was no problem because in that instance the darkness was in front of you where you could see it. You weren't afraid of something hiding in the darkness. You were afraid of the darkness itself. What's more, even the darkness itself didn't bother you if it was in front where you could see it. But at night when you turned out the lights, the darkness would have been behind you. There was no telling what it might get up to. You would walk down the well-lit empty hall to get to the switch, flip it and turn back to go up the stairs. There was light at the top of the stairs but the darkness was behind you. You could feel the darkness chasing you right up the stairs. You ran. You tried to walk but soon enough, you ran. You ran every time. We could hear you all the way upstairs. You could feel the darkness flooding up the stairs behind you. It felt like panic. Nonetheless we made you turn off the light. You had to. No one else was down there. If you didn't do it before you came up, we made you go down again and do it. You protested but you never threw a fit or anything. As it

97

turned out, you were more afraid of looking like a jerk than dealing with the dark. Besides, it worked. You got over your fear of the dark. You wouldn't want to be afraid of the dark now, would you? Ray said, sitting on the rock and looking out over the cactus in the wash below.

When you were a kid, Ray said, you used to walk in your sleep. You did it in the middle of the night. In the morning, we used to find you all over the house, sleeping. We thought you were nuts but you never raised a ruckus. We thought you'd grow out of it. But this one time, you went on this trip with a bunch of other kids. It was exciting for you. You flew on a plane. You stayed in a hotel. In the middle of the night you got right out of bed and went wandering around in the hall. After a while, you started crying. But you weren't just crying, you were crying *without remorse*. You were crying hard enough to wake up every other kid in the hotel. All of the other kids came out of their dark rooms to blink in the light of the hallway. And there you were—this kid in his pajamas crying his guts out in front of the door to the fire escape. At first, you didn't see the other kids, but when you did, it got worse. You really let out all the stops, crying there in front of the door. It was clear what the problem was. One look into your face made it clear as day. You were lost. You didn't know where you were. You had no idea who those other kids were. You didn't know how you got there. You didn't know what was going to happen next. That's why you were crying. After a while a big person showed up and brought you around. It took longer than you might think. All the kids could still hear you crying in your room for some time. In fact, the big person never did bring you around. He just put you to sleep. And in the morning, all the kids crowded around you wanting to know what happened. But you didn't have a clue. You didn't remember anything.

You know what I think? Ray said, looking out over the cactus in the wash. I think you were two kids. I think there was one kid who walked around during the day, and this other kid who walked around at night. I think something got screwed up and both kids ended up in the same body. Yours. From the very moment of conception, I think, there had been these two kids occupying the same body. And when the body was born, there were still two kids—one that was awake all day and the other that only woke up at night. We thought we had one kid but now I know we really had two. One of the kids was as normal as anyone else—being awake all day and sleeping at night. The other kid—his whole life spent half-awake, wandering around in the dark—was probably a bit retarded. But he'd be able to manage. After all, all he'd have to do was find his way back to sleep. Night after night, he'd wake up in the dark and find his way back to sleep. That's not too hard, and it would get even easier with practice. The daytime kid would do all the work involved with growing up and living and growing old etc. The other kid would just have to learn to sleep. I don't know what happened to the daytime kid, but you know what? Ray said, looking out over the cactus in the wash below. *You* are that other kid.

But that's not what I wanted to tell you, Ray said, looking out over the cactus in the wash below. That's just for the sake of neatness. I'm not like you. I don't like to leave a mess. I don't mean clothes and food—your mother takes care of that. I mean thinking about the next guy. I don't like leaving anything behind for the next guy to take care of. I always take care of it myself and I always take care of it right away. If I take something apart, I always put it back together again. If I open something up, I always make sure to close it again before I leave. Even if I find

99

something already open, before I leave, I close it up. It's not my job but I close it up anyway. I always do it myself and I always do it right away. It's a matter of respect. It's a matter of respect for the guy who comes after. You're another kettle of fish altogether. You take care of your clothes and food all right, but as for everything else? You open up everything you come across and it never occurs to you to close it up again before you leave. If you come across a closed situation, you open it up. If the situation is already open when you get there, you open it up more! Closed situations drive you crazy. Closed situations drive you nuts. You have no respect for the guy who comes after. For you there *is* no guy who comes after. I've always found open situations and I've always closed them up. Then I left. But you, you've always found closed situations and you've always opened them up. Your life has been a succession of closed boxes and you've opened every one. Just like my life has been a succession of open boxes and I've closed every one. That's what I do, close boxes. That's what you do, open them up. When there are no more closed boxes for you to open, that'll be it for you. Just as when there are no more open boxes for me to close, that'll be it for me. The last thing I see on this Earth will be a field strewn with closed boxes. The last thing you see will also be a field strewn with boxes, but in your case, every one of those boxes will be open. But that's not what I wanted to tell you; *this* is what I wanted to tell you, Ray said looking at me for the first time.

No one is going to save you, Ray said, looking at me for the first time. That's what I wanted to tell you. I waited a long time I know. I hoped you would figure it out for yourself or if you didn't, I hoped someone else would tell you. But no one told you and you hadn't figured it out for yourself, so I called. You came and I'm telling you now: no one is going to save you.

100

Your mother is not going to save you, and neither am I. It's not our place to save you, and even if it were our place to save you, we couldn't. We can't even save ourselves. Look at this place!— Ray gestured widely—We have not been saved! We did everything we could but here we are anyway. No one could save us, and we couldn't save ourselves. We can't save you, and you can't save yourself. All your secret women can't save you either. Or all your secret men. Your wife with her nightmares is not going to save you. Neither are your children. Not the ones you had or the ones you didn't have. How could they? And quite frankly, I don't think God is interested. God can't save you, or rather, He won't. Why should He? If He were going to save you, He would have already done it. Nope, you are pretty much screwed. That is to say, damned. I wanted to tell you. I wanted you to know. I didn't want you to go on without knowing. That is, I didn't want you to go on like an animal, Ray said sitting on a rock and looking at me for the first time.

Ray had quite clearly gone off his head, I thought, standing out on the porch in front of my raving father. In fact, watching him closely, I couldn't help but notice his head beginning to separate ever so slightly from his body. His head had been bobbing around a bit unnaturally for some time, and now, I couldn't help but notice a minute space opening up across the base of his neck. There it was! I could even glimpse a bit of cactus and sand through it. Ray quite clearly was going off his head in a major way. But even that didn't shut him up, I thought, standing in front of my raving father.

Animals don't have a clue, Ray said as his head began to separate from his body. Animals crawl on and on across the ground without a clue about what's in store for them. They're born, they scratch around for a while and then it's all over—and all that

101

time they are being born and scratching around, they don't have a clue. Animals scratch on and on through their time *in ignorance.* It's the ignorance that makes them animals. Burrowing animals—like moles, for example, or badgers or gophers—burrow through the earth, but all animals burrow through time. Even birds. Even people. And all the while these animals—and some people, even a lot of people, even most people—are burrowing through time, they are burrowing in ignorance. You think moles are blind down there in the darkness and they are. But not just moles, birds and people are blind too. The moles dig around through the earth; people and birds dig around through time. In every case, the animal is blind; in every case, the animal is ignorant. You've been around. You've been all over the place. What's more, you've been all over the place and come back. But everywhere you've been and everything you've seen has been in your tunnel—the tunnel you were burrowing through time. You might as well have stayed home. You don't have to move an inch to burrow through time. You can sit still. You can sit absolutely still—like a boulder—and not move an inch from where you are sitting but still you are burrowing through time, and what's more you are burrowing in ignorance. I couldn't let it go on. It got to me. I couldn't stop thinking. I couldn't stop thinking: there he is, my boy, digging through time as blind as a mole and he's digging in ignorance. He needs to know, I thought. He needs to know as soon as possible. I can't put it off any longer, I thought. I can't stand it any longer, I thought. So I called. I called myself; your mother was in the background. I called. You came. I've told you, Ray said, his head bobbing and plunging a good six inches above his shoulders. I could see the cactus in the wash quite clearly through the space between his bobbing head and his shoulders. His neck seemed to have disappeared completely.

Jesus! What happened to him?

A man pushed through the glass doors to join us on the porch. It was the guy from the plane. Lillian trailed behind him. The man gestured at Ray. Or rather, he gestured at Ray's headless body, still sitting on the rock. His head had shot off into the air. It shot off at such velocity I couldn't follow its trajectory. I thought I had seen Ray's head for a moment high up in the air directly above me but then I lost it in the sun.

That's what you call a "freak accident," the man said, taking a seat at the table. You gave me your card on the plane, remember? I called your wife. She said you'd be here. That must've been your dad, huh?

He said he knew you, Lillian murmured, still standing in front of the door.

Something like this doesn't happen every day, said the man at the table. This is one for the record books. As soon as you recover from your grief, you should write the whole thing down and send it to Ripley. Actually, and don't take this the wrong way, but I think you are going to have a hard time grieving over a death like this. He is dead, isn't he?

The man stepped over to Ray's body and poked it gently with his index finger. The body slumped off the rock.

A heart attack, sure. A stroke, no problem. Cancer? Who wouldn't grieve over that? But spontaneous and propulsive decapitation… ? That's a toughie. They'll never explain that one, but even if they did, it won't make any difference. An event like this throws the very idea of grieving right out the window, the man said.

I heard a distant but resonant thump from someplace way out there in the wash.

I certainly had no intention to walk into this, the man said. I can feel my hair turning white already. I don't think I'll ever get over this. I don't know what to make of this at all. I just wanted my Dictaphone back.

Something started whirring in my trouser pocket.

Yep, you got it, the man said. I can hear it from here. It just goes to show you. Some things you should just let go. You stole it from me twice. I should have let it go. I wanted it for the funeral, but I should have just taken the hint. If I were meant to have that Dictaphone at the funeral, I wouldn't have let it get away from me to begin with. I didn't really need it. It's not like it was a pacemaker or something. I just wanted it. But I should have left well enough alone. I thought the first time I ran into you it was a good omen, but when you managed to get away with it again, I should've taken the hint. This isn't a good omen. This is as far from a good omen as it's possible to get. This isn't even a bad omen. This is an *anti-omen*. Everyone likes to follow through, but it's possible to follow through too much. Sometimes you should just pick up your jacks and go home. I didn't deserve this from you, buddy. The Dictaphone was mine, after all. It wasn't right for you to take it; and it wasn't right for you to lead me into *this*! You *gave* me your food on the airplane. I didn't *take* it. Besides you couldn't eat it. You couldn't eat it because you're sick. Jesus! Look at your knee? It's disgusting.

I had been scratching my knee like crazy. The blood was running down my leg and into my socks.

And you know what? I don't think you're just sick in your skin, the man said, pointing at my knee. I think you're sick in your head. I think you're just plain out of your mind. But that's not my problem. I'm here now and I want the Dictaphone back. Hand it over. I've had enough of you. I've got a funeral to go to, and I'm taking that with me. That's right. It's in your pocket. Christ! You got blood all over it. Just put it on the table. Ma'am, do you have a washcloth? I need something—

There was a loud buzz and the tape ran out with a click. I stuck the machine back in my bag and pushed on through the wash.

It's got to be here someplace, I thought, walking through the wash, searching the ground. I heard it land from the porch. Granted, falling at that velocity, it would've made a loud noise, but the noise couldn't have gone on forever. Nonetheless I'd been spiraling around the house in ever-larger circles for hours, and I still hadn't found it. I heard it. It hit the ground with a thump. I heard the thump, evidently from some distance. It must have been falling at an extremely high velocity to make such a penetrating noise. It must have been falling like a meteor. There should be a crater around here someplace, I thought. There should be a crater and at the bottom of the crater, there should be whatever remains of Ray's head. It might not be much, I thought. It might be only a cinder or maybe an ear. That would be hard to spot. But I should be able to spot the crater. Besides no matter what was left—even a cinder or an ear or the tip of his nose—it wouldn't be right to leave it out here. It wouldn't be right to leave it out here for the animals.

This is completely crazy, I thought, walking through the wash, scanning the ground. Here I am trying to close up a situation Ray has opened. All my life I opened the situations Ray had closed but now I'm trying to close up a situation Ray has opened. If I could leave this situation open, you can bet I would. If I could leave it for the next guy, I would leave it for the next guy, but I can't leave it for the next guy because there is no next guy. In fact, I'm the next guy. When I was a kid, I had this dream. I had the same dream more than once. It was a recurring dream. No matter how many times I had it, I always had it again. It wasn't a scary dream at first, but as time went on, it became scary. What's more, the more I had the dream, the scarier it became. Finally, it was a nightmare, and the nightmare was this: I'm following someone but no matter how quickly I walk, I never catch up, and no matter how slowly I walk, that person never gets away. If I'm here, that person is up there. If I'm up there, that person is even further ahead. If I'm brushing my teeth, that person is having breakfast. If I'm having breakfast, that person has left the house. Wherever I go or whatever I do, that person goes the same place and does the same thing but he does it *before* me. I can't get rid of this person no matter how much I want to, and at the same time I can't catch up to this person though that's the very last thing I want. At some point, I might want to catch up to him as a kind of relief—a relief from all that following. In hopes of obtaining relief, I might skip through everything to get to the very last thing I wanted, but even then it wouldn't happen. I can't meet the person because the person is never here. I can't lose the person because the person is always there. The distance between us is fixed, I thought, walking through the wash, scanning the ground.

It's like the right hand doesn't know what the left hand is doing, I thought, walking through the wash, scanning the ground. Some animals have eyes that move independently. One eye looks at one thing and the other eye looks at something else. Iguanas do that. And you can bet their brains aren't big enough to put the two images together. No way. There's no iguana out there living in this supra-dimensional visual field in which whatever is going on, say, behind it and to the left is synthesized with whatever is going on, say, above it and to the right. Iguanas aren't that smart. If iguanas were that smart, they wouldn't be iguanas. The fact is iguanas just don't care. Why should they? What iguanas care about are bugs. If a bug shows up in one eye, the iguana eats it up. If it shows up in the other eye, the iguana does the same thing. The relationship between what one eye sees and what the other sees simply doesn't enter into the picture. It's a bit schizophrenic but as long as the bugs are forthcoming, why should an iguana care about that? It's a bit like multiple personalities. It's a bit like sleepwalking.

It's like Jui and her sister, I thought, walking through the wash, scanning the ground. When I was younger, I went to a whole slew of far away places. Most of these places turned out to be hot and dry, but the first far away place I went was hot and wet and things grew everywhere. It was part of an exchange program. The deal was I went to the hot wet country, and the hot wet country sent someone here. I stayed in Jui's house. Besides Jui and her parents, there were three girls and a boy. I had a room to myself. The walls of the room were like paper. Jui spoke English. Jui said she had three sisters but actually there were four. The fourth lived in an asylum. She was too loud to keep in the house and god knows what she'd be up to. For a long time I didn't know she existed. Then she came to visit. No one told me but I heard her. I heard her in the middle of the night. The walls were like paper but even if they hadn't been I would have heard her. It was late but I was up. I couldn't sleep. I often couldn't sleep in that house. It was hot and the cockroaches got to me. Generally, it was the cockroaches that kept me up. It was a hot wet place. There were cockroaches everywhere. The mother gassed the place every day but at night they always came back. She gassed my room with strong stuff and came back later and swept the bodies into a wastebasket with a dustpan. She used strong stuff but it didn't always kill them. Sometimes a cockroach would come out of its poisoned swoon just as I was drifting off to sleep. It would come out of its swoon and try to get out of the wastebasket. I would hear it climbing, and I would hear it fall back into the basket. The plastic bag rustled. The cockroach would keep climbing and it would keep falling back. It never quite made it. I was up listening for cockroaches when I heard this crazy girl. Her voice was full of agony and rage. She sounded like she was giving birth. Then she laughed. I didn't know what to make of it. I didn't know this girl existed. Naturally, I thought it was Jui. I let it go on for some time, waiting for someone to intervene. Finally I got up and made my way across the hall. I knocked on the door. Jui opened the door and there behind her on the bed in the lamplight was her sister. She looked right at me and laughed like a maniac. In fact, she was a maniac. I went back to bed. The crazy sister stopped screaming but I could still hear her and Jui whispering. Mostly, they were quiet, gentle people. They spoke a quiet gentle language. I couldn't make out a word though I studied hard. In any case, in spite of everything, it put me right to sleep. No one said a word the next day. Jui only explained it to me weeks later after we had become lovers. We had just hung around on the couch until everyone else had gone to bed. We became lovers and then she told me about her crazy sister. Jui was the gentlest woman I had ever known. For me, the romance was mostly passive. I don't know what she was thinking. I was seventeen. In truth, I liked her friend. She had this friend that went with us everywhere. I liked her. But that just wasn't in the cards. Jui was in the cards. I lived with Jui and her three sisters and the older brother. She spoke English. Looking back, I figure that's what they got out of it—the family I mean. They put me up for a summer and in return Jui got English practice. As the oldest and the ugliest, she would need it because she was going to have to work. The other girls didn't care. Someone was sure to marry them. People were nuts for English in that place. If you knew English in that place, you had it made. The country was hot and wet and everything grew everywhere but still it was poor. In fact one part of the country had already gone dry. The people in that part were reduced to eating bugs. They ate bugs and frogs and just about anything they could get their hands on. They were famous for it. Jui's family wasn't poor but they worried. Before I left, Jui's mother was worried that Jui had gotten pregnant. The walls were like paper in that place. Still, that they knew Jui and I were lovers hadn't occurred to me until that moment. Jui's mother spoke of the problem in general. She talked about men leaving women behind. She talked about men leaving women behind with children. Jui translated. She was much older than me but her voice was much younger. The way things had happened, I knew that was not possible. I didn't say anything. It was embarrassing to talk about it even in that round about way. I let it go. I got on a plane and left. On the plane out, just as the wheels bumped up off the tarmac, I felt more relieved than I had ever felt in my whole life. There were two weird German guys with long blond hair braided like Vikings sitting next to me. They were speaking German together. I still remember them exactly. Sitting on the plane, dizzy with relief, I knew I'd never go back there and I never did, I thought, walking through the wash, scanning the ground.

I'll feel relieved when I find Ray's head, I thought, walking through the wash, scanning the ground. Finding Ray's head is the tricky part, I thought. The rest should go like clockwork. Once I've found the head, putting it back should be easy. When I've got the head, I'll have achieved the grounds for hope. I'll have achieved the grounds for reasonable expectation. With the head in hand, putting it back and closing off the situation should follow naturally. Unfortunately I didn't have the head, and without the head I had nothing. Even without the head, the situation will get closed up eventually, I thought. You can bet on that. Everything gets closed up eventually. Everything gets closed up or it gets buried. If I can't find the head and close up the situation myself, someone else will find the head and close up the situation. If no one finds the head and closes off the situation, the situation—head and all—will still get buried. Time will take care

110

of that. There is no situation so open that time can't bury it, sooner or later. I'm not worried about that. I'm worried about me. I don't want to be in the situation when someone else closes it off. I don't want to be in the situation when it gets buried. I don't want to be buried. I don't want be closed off. The head's got to be around here somewhere. The head is here to be found, but that doesn't mean I'll find it. I often miss things when I'm looking for them, even when they are right under my nose. I might have missed Ray's head already. You can say something is hard to miss and you would be right, but nothing is impossible to miss. If I've missed Ray's head already, the chances I will eventually come across it are virtually nil. The more you overlook something—even something right under your nose, *especially* something right under your nose—the more likely you are to continue to miss it. If you continue to miss it forever, you say it's lost. It's gone. It disappeared. In fact, it hasn't moved. It's not gone at all. It's right where you left it—right under your nose. It's the person who would have found it that's lost. The person who would have found it had his chance but every time he missed it that chance became smaller and smaller. Eventually that person who found it just isn't there anymore. A lost person is there instead. A lost person looking for a lost thing.

I met someone else in the place where Jui and her family lived, I recalled, walking through the wash, scanning the ground. I met him because I had read his books. I was a student. I read his books and then I went to meet him. I met him in a room that was filled with paper. The paper came from all the books. There was paper everywhere. It was all the paper he filled up to write his books. When I came to see him, this man looked harassed. In that place, if you wrote books, you were harassed. Soldiers harassed you and other people harassed you. This man had been harassed. When he wasn't being harassed, he was being ignored.

111

He wrote the books and the whole time he was writing them he was harassed. When he got finished, he was both harassed and ignored. He didn't like the harassment and he didn't like being ignored. When I met him, he was finished with his books and he was finished with being harassed and he was finished with being ignored. He wasn't old but he was finished. I wanted to talk to him about his books, but he said, I have nothing. But you have *this*, I said, gesturing widely at all the paper. I have nothing, he said. I didn't know enough of his language to argue with him about it, and besides even then, somewhere in there, I knew he was absolutely right, I thought, walking through the wash, scanning the ground.

I looked up. The sun was going down. It was going down fast. I hadn't found the head. The place where Ray used to live was miles away now. I could see it below me. The way I had been circling I was almost always above it or below it. I was circling around the house, spiraling outward. The house was at the very foot of the mountain, so half the time my spiraling took me up further and further into the foothills and the other half it took me down, further and further into the wash. Relative to the house where Ray used to live, I was moving in a clockwise direction. I tried to keep the house on my right. I didn't want to get lost. At the moment, I was above the house—that is in the foothills—but the arc had peaked and presently I would be heading back down into the wash. I hadn't found the head yet. I hadn't even spotted a crater. It was getting dark. You would think finding a crater would be the same thing as finding the head. There couldn't be too many craters around here—especially recent craters. It was hard to think of a recent crater as a common thing—to say nothing of a crater with a head in it, or what remained of a head. But who could say? The guy from the plane thought the manner of Ray's death was one in a million, but he might be wrong. A lot of people were dying in this neighborhood. Maybe some of them died in the same manner. If they did, you can bet no one would say a word about it. I certainly had no intention of advertising the manner of Ray's death. I wanted to close the situation off, not open it up—at this point. Who wouldn't? It might be that there was more than one crater with a head in it out here. There might be thousands. There might be an entire plain filled with row after row of craters. I've seen that somewhere. It might have been on the plane. In that case, I wouldn't just have to find the crater with a head in it but also have to make sure the head (in the crater) had belonged to Ray. That was completely beyond me. It didn't bear thinking about.

I'm glad I brought this flashlight, I thought walking through the wash, scanning the ground. If I didn't find the head in the last few remaining moments of daylight, I would have to find it in the dark. It would be difficult to find it in the dark but not impossible with a flashlight. Flashlights are supremely handy instruments. With a flashlight, you can see in the dark. The only drawback to flashlights, or my flashlight anyway, was that the narrow focus of the beam only lets you see one thing at a time. You can see in the dark but you can only see one thing at a time. It wasn't going to be easy to find the head in the dark but at least, with the flashlight, it would be possible, I thought, heading down out of the foothills, scanning the ground.

The wash turned pinkish and then gray and then black. I turned on the flashlight. I could see a cactus, a rock, gravel, stiff grass. Every once in a while, I caught the glow of the eyes of animals here and there among the plants. Rabbits or raccoons or maybe coyotes, I thought. I didn't see any lizards. I didn't see any birds. I didn't see any people. There were people around I knew but they were all sitting out on their front porches. This place was filled with people sitting out on their front porches. All these people were old. This was a place for old people. In general, the weather was great. They came here for the weather and they came here to die. Old people appreciate good weather. In fact, all the old people, out on their front porches, drinking, were appreciating the weather right now. It was a beautiful evening. Not hot. Not cold. Some breeze. No moon but a ton of stars. I was getting deep into the wash and from my angle I couldn't see them. I just saw light glowing around the spaces where their front porches were. But I could hear them. Occasionally I could hear the clink of glasses or a scrap of conversation. They were all out there. All the old people were out there above me and around me sitting on their front porches drinking and talking up a storm, gazing out across the wash. You could bet they could see me. Or rather they could see the beam of the flashlight, groping around down here in the wash. It would look like a finger, I thought, deep in the wash, scanning the ground.

It's hard to find something with a finger, I thought, deep in the wash, scanning the ground. It's hard to find something by touch alone. At night I'm always groping at my bedside. I'm always looking for something with my hands in the dark. It might be my glasses or the clock or a pill or a glass of water. In some cases, I find whatever I'm looking for lickety-split. In others, I never find it. I grope around for quite a while with my hand on the table. I grope around long enough to feel sure that I have explored every inch of the surface. But even though whatever it is I'm looking for has not moved an inch from the table, I still don't find it. In that situation, I have to turn on the lights. There's no other option. If I really want whatever it is that I'm looking for I have to turn on the lights. Even if, at that point, I don't really want whatever it was I was looking for, I still have to turn on the lights just to see where it is. Going back to sleep and

114

forgetting about it is impossible at that point. When I can't find something by touch alone, I become compelled to turn on the lights to see just exactly where that thing is and I do so every time. I roll my body out of bed, walk over to the door and turn on the light, come back to the table and sure enough there it is whatever I couldn't find sitting there on the table just where it's always been. Then I can sleep, I thought, moving down further and further into the wash, scanning the ground with my flashlight.

I wish someone would turn the lights on out here, I thought, scanning the ground with my flashlight. The flashlight worked OK, but I could only see one thing at a time. I wanted to see everything at once. I wish there were some big light somewhere and that someone would turn it on. I'm sure with the lights on the crater with Ray's head in it would stick out like a sore thumb. Unfortunately, there's no light that big and even if there were, it wouldn't help because all the bumps and hills and houses and cactuses would get in the way. If the crater weren't right in front of me, I wouldn't be able to see it. It would be out there somewhere sticking out like a sore thumb in the glare of that huge light but I wouldn't be able to see it because it would be on the other side of something—a hill, a cactus, a rock, a house. A big light—turned on to illuminate the crater with Ray's head in it sticking out like a sore thumb—would only help me if I were above it all. But I wasn't above it all. In fact, I was deep into the wash at this point and getting deeper all the time. But even if I were up in the foothills I wouldn't be above it all, I'd be in the foothills and things would still get in the way.

I was getting thirsty. I hadn't put any water in the bag because I never thought I'd be out here this long. I only took the flashlight and the Dictaphone. I thought, leaving the porch, finding Ray's head would be a snap. I didn't even take any snacks though Lillian had offered them. I don't know what she would do with them now. When I left the porch, she didn't look anywhere near in a mood to eat. In fact, she hadn't looked like she'd be eating anything for some time. She had looked a bit stunned. She looked unresponsive, as they say. In fact, she hadn't managed to say a word after Ray's accident except to offer me snacks and even that she did in a mumble. I had grabbed my bag with the flashlight, stuffed the Dictaphone in it and was climbing over the wall when I caught Lillian's stunned gaze. I said, I'm going to go out and find it. And Lillian mumbled, you should take some snacks, and she drifted through the glass doors to the kitchen to get them but I was over the wall before she came back. I wish I had those snacks now and I wish I had some water. My legs were killing me. Blood from the wound on my knee had run down and crusted in the hair on my shin. I was ungodly tired. Suddenly I felt terribly alone. I stopped scanning the ground. I should have been directly below the house where Ray had lived. I shined the flashlight up out of the wash in hopes of identifying that house. I hoped to spot a porch with a woman sitting at it in the dark looking down at me. I hoped that woman would be Lillian. But I had gone too far. All the porches up on the rim of the wash looked the same. What's more the rim of the wash made a circle all around me. It was impossible to say which side of it was higher. I couldn't find the mountains. Evidently, I had wandered into a crater—an immense crater rimmed with identical houses with identical back porches. Some of these porches were lit and others were dark. Old people sat in the lit ones drinking and talking and looking down into the wash. None of those people were Lillian. She wouldn't have turned on the light—not with Ray's headless body slumped there. When I left, she didn't look like she would be able to read for some time. If she were out on the porch, I'm sure she would be out on the porch in the dark.

Besides I'd been out here for hours and even spiraling around the house I'd traveled miles away from it. I started wondering about coyotes. I wondered if they could smell the blood on my leg. I sat down in the sand. Before I knew it, I had fallen asleep and in my sleep, I dreamed:

I woke up. I woke up in the wash exactly where I had fallen asleep. I woke up to the sound of singing. The singing was coming from the rim of the crater. All the old people on their front porches had stopped drinking and talking and started singing—every single one of them. There were no words. The music was soft but ubiquitous. What's more it was getting louder. The lights started going out. One by one, the lights on the front porches winked out. The sky became huge in the darkness and strewn with stars. Though it was impossible from that distance, I could see each and every one of the old people surrounding me on their porches on the rim of the wash. I could see their faces in great detail. I could see their skin. They were looking down on me and singing. At exactly the same moment, all the old people pulled out flashlights and turned them on. The beams from these flashlights ringing the wash converged on a single point far above it and back. It was somewhere up in the mountains. Something up there glinted. Then I woke up.

Come on up here, buddy, a man said. I could see his face in the beam of my flashlight. It was the guy from the plane. He pulled me to my feet, and then he turned his back to me. It's OK, he said. Just climb aboard. I can see that there's no way you are going to make it on your own. Don't worry. You can have the Dictaphone. I came back for your mother. Your mother is waiting for you. I climbed on his back. He held my legs under his arms. My chin rested on the top of his head.

She worries, you know, the man said, hauling me up out of the wash. It wasn't right to leave her sitting up there on the porch with the body. That's why I came back. I could tell you were useless the very first moment I saw you. That's OK. Nobody's perfect. Of course not everyone's useless either. Some of us are not perfect but we still manage to be useful. Then there are others, like you, who are not perfect or useful. In any case, someone had to go back for your mother. We talked quite a bit. Then somebody called. They found your father's head up the mountain. It landed in a good place. That's a miracle. Your mother didn't tell me to come find you, but I could see that she wanted it. She talks a lot, but she rarely says what she wants. She didn't say she wanted me to come find you, but I could tell she did. It was the way she kept looking out here. She told me all about your father, and she told me all about you. You're quite a piece of work aren't you? You have no respect for anything, do you? Some people respect the dead but have no respect for the living. Others respect the living but don't give a hoot about the dead. But you...? You don't respect the living or the dead, do you? She told me about those people you let in her house. She told me about all your girls and she told me about the babies you didn't have. Yep, you are quite a piece of work. Well, nobody's perfect, but you might have at least tried, buddy, the man said, hauling me up out of the wash.

Why I'll bet going after your father's head is near enough to the only thing you've ever really tried, the man said, hauling me up out of the wash. It's true you mucked it up completely, but at least you tried. Why, I've tried all kinds of things. In fact, I've tried everything I could think of. That's the way I am. If I think of something, I just have to try it out. Granted nothing's come through. I've tried hundreds of things, thousands actually, and not a single one has come through. But I've stayed afloat, haven't

I? For some folks, I know, everything they try comes through. Everything comes through and everything makes it. People like that have the golden touch. People like that hardly have to lift a finger before they're swimming in bananas. But for me, nothing comes through and I never make it. You'd think I'd just give up at this point and get in line. But giving up and getting in line is just not in my deck of cards, buddy. I keep trying because I have to. Trying is what I do. It's in the attempt, as they say. Just take this client I had. That whole deal was dead in the water before I even reached the ground. There I was floating up there in that airplane while the very client I was coming to see was packing it in under someone's coffee table. And the deal we had in mind would've made me. In the face of that kind of reversal, you can bet a lot of guys would call it quits before the body was even cold on the carpet. A lot of guys would have headed straight for the barn, as they say. But not me. I'm headed straight to the funeral. There's always something. Where there's life, there's hope, as they say. And if you missed out on the life part, at least there's the funeral. I haven't missed one yet and I can't say I regret it. You have to take the long view, buddy. In the end, you are either there or you are not and if you're not, you either tried or you did not. But if you did not...well, that's it. People who do are different. But I'm telling you, the people who did not are all the same. There are millions of them. There are millions of them shuffling around on top of the world and there are even more millions of them under the ground. The planet is crawling with them and the ground is choked with their bones. Of course the planet is also crawling with the people who do things and choked with *their* bones, but at least, they tried. Are you beginning to see the light, buddy?

119

I hadn't the faintest clue as to what he was talking about, but we were making amazing progress up and out of the wash and it was nice not having to walk.

Take a guy like you, for example, said the man. You take your father's patrimony and flush it right down the toilet. You kick yourself right out of your father's house and keep going. OK, a lot of guys do that. It's not uncommon. Then you come back! What was the point in coming back after you kicked yourself out? Were you looking for the fatted calf? You shouldn't believe everything you read, buddy. As it is, you annihilated everything. You annihilated the guy who stayed home by kicking yourself out, and then you turned right around and annihilated the guy who left by coming right back. Where does that leave you, buddy? Everything has it's anti-thing. That's physics, buddy. Everything has it's anti-thing, and all that is hunky-dory as long as you keep them apart. There's a universe for things, and there's this other universe for anti-things. But when a thing and its anti-thing come together, pop! You have nothing at all. Get the picture?

As far as I was concerned the guy hadn't even begun to make sense, but then again I wasn't really paying attention. I was more concerned with where we were going. In fact, the progress we were making out of the wash was astonishing. At this point, we had already climbed quite a ways up into the foothills. The grade we were climbing had increased to nearly ninety-degrees which made it pretty much impossible to see what was coming next, but I felt certain that we would have to reach a flat place sooner or later and as soon as we did, I planned to hop right off and get some sleep.

There's a point in being consistent is what I'm trying to say, said the man hauling me up out of the wash. If you're consistent, you make your mark. If you are inconsistent, you make a mess. Some people make a mark; others make a mess, and a mess isn't much different than nothing at all. Who's going to clean it up, buddy? Not you. That's for sure. You couldn't clean it up if your life depended on it. You couldn't clean it up even if you wanted to because, let's face it, it's just too late. You've always been just a bit too late, haven't you? From the very beginning, you've always been a couple of minutes behind. You keep thinking you are going to catch up but you never do. You want to catch up, I'll give you that, but you can't. That's the difference between you and me, buddy. Time management. There's only so much of it, you know. You have to manage it carefully. If you had managed it carefully, like me, there would always be a bit left over. I've got the funeral for example. If I had procrastinated my trip by even a day, I would've missed it. As it is, I missed my client but I've still got the funeral. That's the big difference between you and me, the man said. The big difference is that *I'm still alive*, the man said, hauling me up out of the wash.

We topped the incline. The man scrambled over the lip to a wide, flat grassy place. There was a big group of people there gathered around a table covered with snacks. There were paper lanterns hung here and there, rocking in the breeze, throwing weird shadows all over the place. The air was thick with hushed conversation and the buzz and crackle of electric bug zappers massacring mosquitoes like there was no tomorrow. I hopped off the man's back. I spotted Lillian right away. She was all dressed up in a classy black outfit, holding a paper plate in her hand, standing beside a large rectangular hole. So this is what it comes too, I thought. This is it.

But then I heard a scratching noise behind me. I turned around just in time to catch Ray scrambling up out of the wash. He did it more nimbly than I would have thought possible. He was wearing a black suit with what looked like a black carnation in the lapel. I had you going there, didn't I? he said, standing up on the grass. It was just an optical illusion. I tucked my head in like this.

Ray tucked in his head in the manner made familiar by shelled reptilian quadrupeds all the world over.

Lillian drifted around the hole to join us. Thanks for hauling him up here, she said to the man from the plane, who was standing beside me, beaming. I couldn't bring myself to ask you, but that's what I really wanted. It's nothing, ma'am, said the man. These snacks are fantastic, Lillian said to Ray. No cholesterol! She showed the plate to Ray. It was full of asparagus stalks with white gunk smeared all over the tips.

So, who died? I asked, a trifle uneasily. I realized besides refusing the snacks from Lillian earlier, this was the first time I'd opened my mouth in three days. My voice sounded strange.

All the people standing around the snack table turned around at the same time. They were all extremely old. Each wore a big shit-eating grin, and more than half had bits of asparagus and white gunk dripping from the corners of their mouths. No one said a word. The whole scene was a bit ghoulish.

Why don't we just go take a look-see? said Ray, gently taking my elbow in one hand and steering me toward the hole. I'm not sure you really knew him, said Lillian, joining us on the other side. The man who had brought me there looked up and away and then started whistling.

Truth be told, I wasn't too eager to look into the hole. I didn't really need to know who was there—that that person was dead was enough for me. I'd probably never met him anyway. But by the time I realized that, it was too late. We were right there.

Go ahead! Take a look! said Ray. In the rush, we didn't have enough time for a coffin. On the other hand, the body's still in pretty good shape. I'm not sure he even knows this guy, honey, my Lillian said to Ray.

I looked.

But there was no one there. No coffin. No person. Nothing. Just a rectangle of freshly turned soil.

But? I said, turning to Ray and Lillian.

Look closer, Lillian and Ray said at the same time.

I fell backwards into the hole. I won't say I was pushed. In any case, the hole wasn't as deep as it looked. I didn't break anything. It only took me a few seconds to scramble to my feet. When I had brushed myself off, I looked up and saw the hole was already ringed by old faces grinning down at me, and beyond them the night sky crammed full of burning stars.

Oh, so I'm the dead one, is that it? I shouted up out of the hole. I'd really had enough at this point. Too late for me, is it? I shouted. But you forgot all about *this*!

I pulled the Dictaphone out of my bag and held it up to them like a weapon. I could feel it whirring in my hand. Maybe I am and maybe I'm not, I said. But….but…

In truth, I couldn't think of anything else to say. So instead of blabbering on, I just cocked my arm back and threw the Dictaphone straight up toward the sky with as much force as I could muster. I think it cleared the rim but it was hard to tell in the dark. I know throwing it away like that was a pathetic gesture but it was the best I could do under the circumstances. Thank god my children weren't there to see it.